Tales of the Were
Grizzly Cove

Loaded for Bear

BIANCA D'ARC

Copyright © 2018 Bianca D'Arc

ISBN: 1986636941
ISBN-13: 978-1986636940

DEDICATION

To my family. I finished writing this book during a tough time emotionally for us—right around a very sad anniversary in our lives—the anniversary of the loss of my mother. You might say this book gave me something else to focus on that put me in a happier place while writing it. I hope that comes through and that you all enjoy reading this as much as I enjoyed writing it. I truly love Grizzly Cove and if it existed, I'd love to live there.

CHAPTER ONE

Amelia Ricoletti—Mellie, to her friends—ran down the hallway, holding her breath. Billows of smoke followed her, along with the blaring beep of the fire alarm.

"Shit!" she whispered, angry at this latest fumble at potion-making. No way she could hide this failure. She could hear her sister's feet pounding up the stairs from the bookstore to the apartment already.

Sure enough, Urse burst in the door, worry on her face. She waved her hands and said a few words, and the smoke cleared, the siren stopped beeping on the smoke alarm, and Mellie could breathe fresh air again as the windows opened seemingly of their own accord. Urse might be frowning at her, but sometimes, it was good to have a spell-wielding witch around.

Mellie leaned one hand against the back of a chair and sighed in defeat. She'd been so close this time. At least... She'd thought she'd been closer to the right combination of ingredients for the complex spell she wanted to cast through her potion-witchery. The fact that the mess had burst into flames meant she'd been utterly wrong.

Urse came over and put her hand on Mellie's shoulder. "You okay?"

"Yeah." Mellie looked up to meet her sister's eyes, afraid there would be condemnation in her gaze.

They'd both been tasked with making Grizzly Cove safer for the shifters and other magical folk who sought shelter here. So far, Urse had done a bang-up job casting wards that kept evil creatures of the deep away and protecting the waters of the cove itself. Her ward was both permanent and immensely powerful. Everyone agreed Urse had done an amazing thing, and she'd found true love at the same time.

Her older sister was now mated to the Alpha bear, John Marshall, whom many people called simply Big John. Mellie liked her new brother-in-law a lot. He was a good man, and he'd made Urse happier than Mellie had ever seen her. Everything had turned around for Urse. Her life was really great.

It was Mellie's that sucked. She'd been given the simple task of creating a potion that she could put into the water that would hopefully drive the evil leviathan and its minions even farther away from the mouth of the cove. Simple, right?

Yeah… Not so much.

Mellie had been working on this for months now and failing every time. This latest batch had been a rather spectacular failure. It was broad daylight, and everybody had probably seen the billowing smoke coming out of the windows.

Great. Just great. Mellie was quickly becoming the town joke.

"Some all-powerful *strega* I turned out to be," she mumbled.

"Aw, honey…" Urse put her arm around her younger sister's shoulders and squeezed. "It'll work out. You'll find the right recipe. I know it. You're one of the most powerful *strega* in generations. We both are. I do spells and wards, but you, my dear sister, are a potion master. But let's face it. You've taken on probably the hardest problem you'll face in your lifetime. *Roma* wasn't built in a day."

The sisters were of Italian descent and were hereditary witches steeped in the traditions of Italy. They were a special breed of witch, known as *strega*, as had been many generations of women in their family before them. Urse and Mellie had found their niche in Grizzly Cove, and a purpose for their magic-craft. Protecting the people who called this place home had become a mission both sisters shared.

Urse had already done her part. She'd cast powerful, permanent wards around the town and the cove. Nothing of evil intent could cross over that boundary, and it would remain so forevermore. That was Urse's special gift. Her superpower, as Mellie thought of it.

Mellie's own magic was much more prosaic. Kitchen magic, her *nonna* called it sometimes. Mellie instinctually knew which substances to brew together to create powerful potions. She was an herb witch, kitchen witch, or potion witch. There were many names for her rather unglamorous calling.

Urse got to do the fancy chanting and light shows while Mellie got stuck in the kitchen, mixing up batches of noxious stuff. Okay. She wasn't really being fair. The things she cooked up weren't always noxious. In fact, most of the time they were really rather pleasant. Yummy, some of them, or just fragrant and luxurious.

Mellie created all sorts of balms, salves, elixirs and tonics. She'd also learned how to create her own skincare lotions and treatments, which saved the girls a bundle on cosmetics, sunblock and moisturizers. It was only when her potions were brewed with specific intent—as in this case—that they sometimes tended toward the explosive.

"At least the fire department didn't show up this time," Mellie mused, trying to raise her own spirits. She'd never get it right if she kept being so depressed about her failures.

They both heard the heavy tread of feet up the stairs that led to the apartment above the bookshop. There were at least two of the big bear-men on their way up at a fast clip. That meant it wasn't just John, coming to pick up Urse early.

"Um..." Urse looked chagrined as a loud knock sounded on the door, followed by a query.

"Everything all right in there?"

The voice didn't belong to Urse's mate, John. Nope. This particular bear shifter was easy to identify by his light Russian accent. Peter. Grizzly Cove's newest deputy, owner of the butcher shop and part-time fireman. Mellie's own personal nightmare because of the way she kept making a fool out of herself in front of the man.

Mellie groaned and hid her head in her hands while Urse went to answer the door. She let them in. At least it wasn't the full team this time. Just Peter and Sheriff Brody, who was hefting a large red fire extinguisher.

"I know John installed a few of the smaller extinguishers up here, but I grabbed this out of the station when I saw the smoke coming out of your windows. Is the fire out?" Brody asked, moving into the apartment and heading down the hall toward the room Mellie had turned into her laboratory-slash-spell chamber.

"Don't cross the threshold!" Mellie shouted after him. "There wasn't really that much fire. Just a bad reaction that produced a lot of smoke." She caught up with him just outside the door and scooted in front of him. "It might not be safe for you in there," she warned him as Brody scowled.

"Why not?" Brody looked instantly suspicious. He was the town's sheriff. She supposed he had a right—and a predisposition—to be wary.

Mellie looked at Peter. Maybe he could help explain this in a way that wouldn't get Brody mad at her.

"I had him under magical sedation, but the smoke must've woke him up, and his tail twitched, stirring the contents of the cauldron before it was ready," she explained to Peter, who was the only one aware of the lengths she'd gone to for her ingredients.

Peter stepped forward. "Is he on the loose in there?"

She cringed. "Maybe."

"Is *what* on the loose in there?" Brody nearly shouted.

Mellie looked back at the sheriff. "A komodo dragon," she admitted. "A big one."

"Mellie!" her sister chastised her, frowning.

"The ancient potion grimoire Nonna sent said I needed dragon blood. I figured a komodo dragon was the best I could do under the circumstances, and believe me, that wasn't easy to get. Peter had to source this guy from a private collection, and he's only on loan. We have to get him back before the owner misses him."

"Is it dangerous?" Brody turned to Peter.

"Not really." Peter frowned and stepped forward. "Is the room otherwise safe?" he asked Mellie.

"Yeah. The potion didn't work. It fizzled and caused a lot of smoke, but the reaction is spent. The only thing dangerous in there now is the lizard," she told him.

"I'll take care of the animal," Peter told Brody, and the sheriff backed off, but only by a few feet. He put himself in front of Urse and looked like he wanted to protect Mellie, as well, but she refused to back down. This was her problem, after all. She'd created it. She'd damn well help resolve it.

Peter opened the door slowly, and a little residual smoke puffed out around their feet. As the door swung wide, Peter launched himself, quick as a shot, into the room, moving almost too fast for Mellie to follow. He was on the floor, wrestling the giant lizard into its cage when she finally got a good look.

"Why did you have to let it out of the cage?" Brody asked as he watched Peter work. He'd come closer, to stand at her side.

"I needed its blood. I had to have access to get a needle into him. Plus, I had it under control magically until the bad reaction from the potion wrecked all the magic in the room. It was asleep. Docile." She shrugged, watching as Peter won the battle to get the animal into its large cage.

Peter stood and dusted himself off. "Do you still need blood from this creature or can I return him?"

Mellie shook her head. "You can take him back. His blood didn't work for this potion, and frankly, I'm at a loss to figure out what to do next. I either have to try something else or find an actual dragon." She chuckled morosely. "So…something else, it is. Only, I'm not sure there is anything left to try. I've been working on this forever. I've tried everything I know, and nothing's right."

Dammit. She was whining in public. She didn't want the men to know how close to insanity this little project was driving her. She clamped her lips together and refused to say anything else. She'd said quite enough already, thank you very much.

Urse came over and put an arm around her shoulders, walking her back down the hallway toward the living room. Urse understood. She'd been Mellie's confidant all her life. Urse had been trying to help Mellie, but it was no good. This was Mellie's task. She had to find the answer on her own…and she had to find it soon. She was letting everyone down each day she struggled to find the answer to the problem that had been set before her.

Urse had already done her part and made the town and cove safe. Now, it was up to Mellie to move the leviathan and its minions farther away, if she could, so that the fishing boats could go outside the protected waters of the cove. So that the mer folk could once again hunt in the ocean. So that the magical folk living along the coast would be safe from the evil prowling along the shoreline just outside the mouth of the cove.

Peter came down the hall, followed by Brody, who eyed the cage as if it might independently open and let loose a pissed off komodo dragon to rain terror down on Mellie's apartment. It would be funny, if Mellie wasn't feeling so morose. Of course, she noticed the way Peter's muscles bulged as he carried the heavy animal crate like it weighed nothing at all. Bear shifters were strong, and Peter seemed stronger than most.

Mellie might be feeling blue, but she'd have to be dead not

to notice scrumptious Peter as he walked past, heading for the staircase. Brody was with him. He nodded at them before he followed Peter out of the apartment.

"Well, there goes that attempt, complete with public humiliation. I'm really batting a thousand lately." Mellie spoke her thoughts, no longer censoring herself. It was only her and Urse now, and her sister knew how difficult Mellie was finding this mission.

"Not that public. I don't think Brody would tell anyone other than John—and then, he'll probably only mention the exotic lizard. You know John doesn't spread tales. Your Peter won't talk either."

"He's not *my* Peter," Mellie protested sulkily.

"Are you sure he knows that?" Urse asked, arching one eyebrow.

"Pfft." Mellie made a shooing motion with her hands at her sister.

While it was true she had been attracted to Peter from almost the first moment she'd seen him, he hadn't really given her any indication that he felt the same. Much as she wanted to attract his attention, Mellie was also in the midst of what could be the most important spell work of her life—and failing miserably. This was no time to start dating a new guy.

She had to keep her eye on the ball. No time for distractions. The entire town was counting on her, not to mention the colony of mer folk in the cove and all the innocent creatures out at sea just beyond the border created by Urse's powerful ward.

Urse had done *her* job. Easy peasy. She'd set tremendous permanent wards all around the town, protecting it from all sides, including the waters of the cove itself. An intense magical wall prevented anything with evil intent from swimming in past the mouth of the cove. It also prevented evil beings from entering the town, and much of its environs—including the forest all around them. Urse had done an incredible job.

Mellie? Not so much. In fact, Mellie felt like a total failure in comparison to her older sister. Not only had Urse cast her wards with amazing impact, she'd also managed to capture the heart of the Alpha bear while she was at it. John Marshall—the mayor of the town and the Alpha of this group of bear shifters—was Urse's true mate. Their happiness was beautiful to behold, but it also made Mellie feel a little jealous. Not in a bad way. Just wishing she could find that special something with a special someone, like her sister had.

That Peter… Yeah, he was the kind of man fantasies were made of. He was a bear, but different from the others in town. For one thing, he was Russian, with a faint accent left from the land of his birth. It made him sound exotic to Mellie's American ears. He was also built on the massive side—as were most of the men around town—but Peter was a bit of a giant, even among his friends.

He'd always been a gentle giant with her, though. While Urse had been in danger and spell-crafting for all she was worth, Mellie had been basically under house arrest. The first couple of times Urse went out to cast her spells, she'd warded the apartment so Mellie couldn't get out until Urse came back. The stinker.

Then, when Urse had almost been lured away by the evil song of the leviathan and Mellie had been trapped in the apartment, John had sent Peter over to babysit. His job had been to make sure Mellie didn't try to leave and go help her sister. According to their grandmother, who had a gift of clairvoyance, each of the girls had to do their tasks completely on their own. If one tried to help the other, it could all fail.

That didn't mean Mellie was content to just sit and watch while her sister went into danger time and time again. She'd wanted to be close in case of disaster, so maybe she could help save her sister's life. But the bears of Grizzly Cove weren't allowing it. At Urse's request.

Double stinkers.

Peter had been sent to sit in the apartment with her to make sure she wouldn't circumvent Urse's desires and the Alpha's orders. As if Mellie would deliberately cause problems for her sister. All she'd wanted to do was be nearby, in case everything went wrong and Urse needed her. But no. Urse had decreed Mellie couldn't be anywhere near and had to be watched like some kind of prisoner, under house arrest.

Mellie still hadn't quite forgiven her sister for that. In fact, their relationship had been a bit strained since Urse had saved the cove and Mellie had been failing at every attempt to do her part. It didn't help Mellie's mood that her sister—her best friend—had found her mate and was totally wrapped up in John.

Not that Mellie wasn't happy for them. She was. She really was. John was a great guy, and Mellie couldn't have asked for anyone better for her only sister. It's just that seeing them so happy… When Mellie was failing so badly every time she tried to brew a potion… It was hard. Urse wasn't there in the middle of the night when Mellie needed to talk.

Urse had moved out of the apartment above the bookstore and moved into John's house—his den—farther up the cove. She wasn't all that far away, but she wasn't *there* for Mellie the way she always had been. Mellie was having a rude awakening about just how much she'd come to depend on her older sister. She hadn't realized it, but she was coming to appreciate it now more than ever.

Mellie was feeling lonely and a little left out of her sister's life. She knew it was a bit selfish to feel like that, but she couldn't help it.

"Here." Urse set a steaming cup of tea down in front of Mellie. She'd been so wrapped up in her own morose thoughts, she hadn't really heard Urse rustling around by the stove, making tea. Chamomile, by the delicate fragrance of it. Yum.

"Thanks, sis." Mellie truly loved her sister, even if she was having a hard time adjusting to the new dynamic of her sister being married.

Urse came over and sat down across from her at the kitchen island, sipping her own mug of steaming tea. She let Mellie enjoy the tea for a moment before she spoke.

"Is there anything I can do to help?" It was the same question Urse had been asking for weeks, but Mellie didn't have a new answer. She just shrugged. "I'm sorry, hon. I really am."

"I know." Mellie sipped her tea again, feeling calmer and a bit sad. "I'm stopping for today. I'll have to clean out the laboratory and bless everything all over again. There's a new moon tonight, so it's a good time to do it. Then, I guess I'll start fresh tomorrow, but I have no idea how. I'm sort of at a dead end here."

"But I thought the grimoire Nonna sent had the potion you needed," Urse said quietly.

"It does. At least, I think it does, but it's so ancient. Some of the ingredients I have to guess at because we don't call them by the names listed anymore. I've had to do a lot of research, and I think I've got everything right, but there's one ingredient—a really important one—that I just don't understand and can't figure out."

"The dragon's blood thing, right?" Urse asked, familiar with the problem Mellie had been kicking around for the past few days. "Are you sure there's not some obscure herb or potion that goes by that name?"

"I've tried everything. I'm at the point where I think there might actually have been dragons around at the time the grimoire was written." Mellie chuckled at the thought. *Real dragons? Yeah, right. Pull the other one.*

"Well, it is pretty old," Urse offered uncertainly.

Mellie looked at her sister in disbelief. "Seriously? You think there really were dragons?"

"Well, you know the old saying. Where there's smoke, there's usually fire. I mean, we have all these old stories about dragons. So, why couldn't they have been real at some point?" Urse shrugged, sounding unsure of her own theory.

"I thought they were just stories ancient people made up when they found dinosaur bones and couldn't explain them," Mellie offered. That idea had always made sense to her.

"I'm not so sure," Urse told her. "I think you should talk

to Lyn Ling tomorrow. There are lots of stories about dragons in China. Maybe she knows something."

"But the grimoire is from Italy," Mellie protested weakly.

"And Marco Polo traveled the silk road," Urse fired right back. "What if there really were dragons in China? Didn't you tell me some of the other potions in the grimoire used ginseng and other Asian herbs?"

"Ginseng also grows in the United States, you know," Mellie said, just to be contrary. She really wasn't in a good mood. Not after this latest humiliation. But she knew Urse was trying to help, so she tried not to be too bitchy.

"Okay. You're proving my point, you know. If the ginseng in the grimoire is from the U.S., then why couldn't it also reference dragons from China? Ancient people traveled and traded, you know. It just took them longer to get where they were going."

Mellie wanted to growl but bit it back. Urse's heart was in the right place, even if Mellie wasn't in the mood to hear it right now.

"I'll go to Lyn's shop tomorrow," Mellie conceded. "Find out what she knows. I promised to bring Daisy some new books anyway."

Urse smiled. "Good. Now, that's settled, I'm heading home." Urse stood and put her empty mug in the sink. "Will you be all right on your own?"

Urse asked her that every afternoon when she headed home from the bookstore they ran together. Mellie would take over for a couple of hours—not that they were inundated with customers, but there always was a chance of someone stopping by—then she'd lock up and retreat to the apartment above the shop to do a little work on her potions before heading to bed.

More often than not, she'd eat dinner all alone. It was getting on her nerves, but she wouldn't tell Urse that. Not for the world. Mellie had always had Urse in her life. They'd cooked together all the time and spent a lot meals laughing and talking with each other. Now, Urse was off doing the happy couple thing, and though she'd invited Mellie to dinner many times, Mellie hadn't wanted to horn in on their newlywed period.

Maybe it would become easier in time, but for now, Mellie was spending a lot of time alone, thinking about how lonely she was. It was circular thinking, she knew, but knowing that didn't always help stave it off.

"Yeah, I'll be fine," she assured her sister. "Go. Tell John I said hi. I'm just going to finish my tea, then I'll head down to the bookstore."

Urse left a few minutes later, and Mellie did as she'd said. She left the mugs in the sink for later and headed downstairs. She would spend an hour on the computer downstairs, doing more research into the ingredients she needed. She spent a lot of time doing research these days.

She was scrolling through a website devoted to dragon lore when the bell above the door to the shop tinkled, breaking her concentration. She looked up to find Peter walking into the shop.

"Back so soon?" Mellie asked, guessing Peter had driven the komodo dragon straight out of town and back to its owner.

"It's been hours," Peter told her. "It's well past your usual closing time. I saw your lights still on and figured I'd stop by to see if everything was okay."

Mellie looked past him to see out the front windows. Son of a gun. It was dark out there. The street lights were on, which meant it was pretty late.

"Wow. I guess I got caught up in my research." She sat back and stretched the kinks out of her lower back. Judging by how much her spine hurt from sitting in one position for too long, she probably had been hunched over the computer far longer than she'd realized.

"What are you researching?" Peter asked conversationally.

He wasn't usually one for small talk, so his question was a little out of the ordinary. Was he making an effort to be more friendly? If so, she was all for it. She'd like to get *really* friendly with him, in fact, but she didn't want to get the cart before the horse. Peter had been a bit aloof with her since Urse had done her work, and Mellie didn't want to chance that he'd scamper off again.

"Dragons, of course," she told him, laughing weakly at herself. "Urse has got me half convinced that there were such things as real dragons once upon a time."

"But there were." Peter's statement set her back. He sounded so certain.

"Seriously? How can you be so sure?"

"There is dragon blood in my family line," he told her.

"Wait. What?" Mellie shook her head, trying to wrap her mind around what he was saying. "You mean dragons like…*shifter*…dragons?" Suddenly, it was as if a light bulb came on in her mind. "Why didn't I think of that before? Dragons were shifters?" She stood and started to pace. "Stars! Do any still exist? Why didn't you mention this before?" She turned her questions on Peter. "You have dragon blood? How far back?"

"My grandmother's grandfather was a dragon, or so she claims. He died long before I was born, of course, and I don't personally know anyone who can shapeshift into a dragon. These days, with the rise of human technology—especially radar—they'd probably be living in secret, in very remote locations, if any still exist. Dragons were hunted, you know. Not just in stories, but in real life. My great-great-grandfather lived in secrecy, too. Only the family knew what he was, and I understand there was great rejoicing when the children of that union all turned out to be bears and not dragons."

Mellie thought hard about what he was saying. "But you still have dragon blood. At least a little. I wonder if I tried the potion with a drop of your blood…"

Peter squirmed a bit, which was unusual for him. "I'm willing to try, but I'm a bear, Amelia. One of my distant ancestors was a dragon, but I don't think that really counts because my animal side is bear all the way. At least, that's how it feels to me."

"Look." Mellie sighed heavily as she moved to stand before him. Her tone and demeanor were as serious as she ever got. "I don't have much choice here but to try. If you're willing, I'd love to give this another shot. Who knows? It might work."

"Or, it might not, and the entire fire department might show up next time," he cautioned her.

She didn't like the reminder of her failures, but he did have a point. She shook her head. A little more embarrassment was a small price to pay. And there was a small chance it could work this time. It was worth the risk.

"That's a chance I'll have to take," she told him. "I've got work to do cleaning out the lab and purifying it tonight when the new moon rises. Come by tomorrow afternoon, and we can start brewing, if you haven't changed your mind."

Peter shook his head, much the way his bear form sometimes did. "I haven't changed my mind. I'm always willing to help you, *zvyozdochka.* I just don't want you to get your hopes up too high. My dragon ancestor is very distant."

"You're the best I've got, Peter," she told him, realizing that was true on many levels.

CHAPTER TWO

Mellie worked long into the night, first cleaning up the mess she'd made earlier with the komodo dragon, then performing ritual cleansing as the new moon rose in the dark sky. She couldn't see it, but she knew it was there. The magic of the moon was something she was very attuned to, as waxing and waning power of the moon in its phases influenced her work all the time.

The next morning, Urse came in, as usual, to open the shop downstairs. They'd agreed that Urse would take the morning shift because Mellie was staying up late each night working on her potions. The sisters would usually have lunch together then work side by side for a while in the shop before Urse went home mid-afternoon and Mellie stayed down in the shop until closing time. Then, she'd go back up to her lab and work on her pet potions.

They'd fallen into a routine over the past few weeks, and Mellie was glad of it this morning, as she got to sleep in, knowing that Urse was taking care of things downstairs. Mellie finally got out of bed a little before noon and made herself presentable. She put lunch on the stove so that it would be ready when Urse flipped the sign from OPEN to CLOSED downstairs and came up to share the mid-day meal.

There was a lot to discuss today, but oddly, Mellie felt reticent about sharing Peter's family secret with her sister. That stopped Mellie in her tracks. She told her sister pretty much everything. Why, now, was she suddenly reluctant to share this?

It was Peter. That had to be it. Mellie had been shy about her growing feelings for the giant werebear because Urse seemed to gain a little too much satisfaction from teasing her sister about it. Mellie's feelings about Peter were special…and private. Not for public consumption or ridicule.

Not that Urse had been mean about it. No, she'd just liked teasing her sister. Not in a cruel way, but in that older-sisterly way that sometimes drove Mellie nuts.

This, though, was a little different. The information Peter had imparted about his family history felt like a secret he had trusted her with. She wouldn't betray that implied trust lightly. So, maybe Urse wouldn't be hearing about the plans Mellie had for tonight with Peter and her potion room. Huh. That was different. She didn't like keeping secrets from Urse, but this felt like the right thing to do. Quite a contradiction.

Mellie didn't have more time to dwell on it, because at that moment, she heard Urse's light tread on the stairs leading up to the apartment. Lunch was just about ready, so Mellie pulled the pan of chicken from the oven and set it on the table, just as the door opened.

"Smells yummy," Urse observed, pausing to give her sister a quick hug hello.

The sisters ate and talked about the town and the people, not going near any of the more difficult topics. Mellie didn't mention Peter at all. Not even to say he was coming over later that day. With any luck, Urse would have left before Peter showed up.

Mellie liked him too much to betray his confidence, and she wouldn't really be able to explain his visit to Urse's satisfaction without explaining about why he was now, suddenly, helping her with the potion. There was a small temptation to let Urse think that maybe Peter and Mellie were dating, or something, but that might be even worse because the teasing would probably know no bounds. Better to keep Peter's involvement to herself for now.

The sisters went back downstairs together, after lunch had been cleared away, to work in the bookstore. They were redecorating the front display windows with a new selection of books. The business was doing surprisingly well considering the small population of the town. Most of the men were readers, though, which helped considerably. Apparently, werebears were more erudite than she would have expected before moving here. No wonder the bookshop had been second only to the bakery in gaining approval from the town council.

That, right there, pointed out the basic priorities of bear shifters in Mellie's mind. First, they liked to eat—especially the sweets that the bakery specialized in, though they also served man-sized sandwiches on freshly baked bread. Right after food came books, for some reason.

She might have thought a gun shop would be the next priority after learning the entire town council and most of the residents had been Special Forces soldiers, but she supposed they were all still well-armed enough without adding any new firepower to their arsenals. Plus, aside from the gun collections all over town, the men could turn into deadly bears any time they wanted. They carried around their own weapons, built into their bodies, in the way of claws and teeth. Quite a few of them were into knives in their human form, as well, and wore them like women wore pocketbooks—with them at all times, an accessory to their lifestyle.

So, the second business to be approved had been a bookstore. Theoretically, all the men in town had officially retired from military service. Most of them didn't follow any kind of schedule anymore. The town was supposed to be an artist's colony, and the men lived a life, not of leisure, but of their own design. They woke when they wanted. Ate when they wanted. Dabbled in art, if that was their thing. And they read. A lot. More than the average person, Mellie thought, though she didn't know precise figures.

Still, the bookshop was doing reasonably well, even in such a small community. Most of the men in town came in at least once every couple of weeks to pick up book orders. The shop wasn't stocking loads of books on spec. It was more boutique than that. Mellie and Urse had decided to cater to their customers. *Specializing in special orders* was fast becoming their motto. If someone wanted a particular book, they just let one of the sisters know, and a few days later, it would arrive.

The floor space in the store itself was devoted to several specialties. There was a section of books about art—helping to maintain the façade that the town was really an artist's colony. Any tourists who might come through and browse in the bookstore would expect that. There was also a section of coffee table books about the Pacific Northwest. There was a cookbook section, and they had just decided to devote a small corner to children's books.

In fact, that's the project they had been working on for the past week. They'd repainted that corner and put up shelves in strategic places to create a little nook perfectly sized for little bodies to browse books shelved at their level. Right now, little Daisy Ling was the only child resident of Grizzly Cove, but as more men paired off with their new mates, the sisters had begun to think ahead.

Mellie silently thought Urse was already planning for her own children with John, but the sisters hadn't really discussed it yet. That was something Urse and John had to figure out between themselves first. Mellie didn't know, for example, if John was in favor of the large family Urse had always wanted. Would he object to the fact that some of their kids could be born without the ability to shift? Some, or all, might be born mages. Mellie knew for a fact that Urse was hoping for at least one little girl to carry on the *strega* tradition.

She'd asked Urse about it when she and John had first gotten together but hadn't pushed for an answer, realizing she was getting a little too nosy. She'd always been able to ask her sister anything, but that was changing now that Urse was mated. Mellie was no longer her sister's primary confidant. John had taken precedence in Urse's life, as Mellie knew was the way it should be, but even so, she couldn't help feeling a little bit left out.

As the afternoon wore on and the children's corner took shape, Mellie began to worry that Peter might show up at any moment. She didn't want to have to explain to her sister why she'd kept silent on the arranged meeting with the hunky Russian bear-man.

Mellie breathed a sigh of relief when Urse came into the main area carrying her coat. Mellie looked up to find John waiting for Urse on the sidewalk. He was talking to Brody, the sheriff of the town and John's right-hand man. As Mellie watched, the two men parted, and John reached for the door handle to let himself into the bookstore.

"Just in time," Urse said as she walked over to her mate. They shared a hug and kiss that Mellie politely looked away from.

"Hi, Mel. How's it going?" John greeted her a few minutes later. Mellie looked up and smiled at her sister's husband. He was a good guy.

"Can't complain," Mellie answered back. "How's the mayor gig working out for you?"

John chuckled at her words. "Same old, same old. Sea monsters. Mermaids. Bears." He shrugged, as if it were all old hat, and Mellie marveled again at the town she now called home.

"And, here, I thought San Francisco was weird." She laughed as she said it. She'd loved growing up near San Francisco and still missed it—especially her nonna, who still lived there—but Grizzly Cove was truly her home now. It felt *right* to be here. Among the bear-men and their mer allies.

Urse and John left a few minutes later, and Mellie breathed

a sigh of relief. Peter would probably show up any time now. She checked her appearance in the small mirror kept on the wall in the backroom. Not that she was vain or anything, but they had been painting and moving books around all afternoon. She didn't want to present herself to Peter, of all people, with bright blue paint streaked in her hair or something.

Peter hesitated to go into the bookstore until he was certain the Alpha and his mate were long gone. He was a private man, who had learned to hide the things that mattered most to him growing up in the Soviet system. That had all been a very long time ago, and things in the motherland were very different now, but old lessons were hard to unlearn.

Peter had been making his home in the United States for several decades, and he still found it hard to take the freedoms here for granted. He'd grown up in a place where everyone was spying on everyone else and backroom deals were a matter of course. Black-market goods. Under-the-table payoffs. Outright bribes and middle-of-the-night raids had been the way to get things done in the old Soviet Union. Grizzly Cove, however, was something completely different.

Everything here was above board and out in the open. For the most part. That's the way the Alpha wanted it, and among the shifters here, that's the way it was. They still had to keep their existence secret from the rest of the world. Humanity wasn't ready to discover a whole colony of bear shifters in their midst. Everyone agreed on that. Humans weren't comfortable with the concept of magic, unless it was just a fairy story for children with no teeth.

The idea that shifter wolves, bears, raptors, big cats and creatures of all kinds lived among them while wearing their human forms would be a tough one to swallow for most humans. The rest of the supernatural world would probably be even harder to deal with. Vampires. Fey. And many other kinds of magical folk.

Then, there were the evil ones. The leviathan chief among

them at the moment. Humans would totally freak out if they knew what was in the water, ready to terrorize the coastline and all the ships at sea. Sadly, while the leviathan was bad enough, Peter knew there were tales of much worse things that could be unleashed by the Destroyer if the worst should happen and she returned to the mortal realm.

He was getting ahead of himself, though. The mission, right now, was to help Mellie in any way he could to push the leviathan farther from shore. According to her clairvoyant grandmother, both of the Ricoletti sisters had a role to play in protecting the cove from the creature and its minions. The older sister had already done her part in a spectacular fashion. Rarely had Peter seen such powerful wards. That they were permanent wards, meant to stand the tests of time, was an unexpected bonus.

Now, it was Mellie's turn, and she was having serious problems coming up with the right ingredients for her potion. She'd discussed her challenges with Peter perhaps more than any other bear. He got the impression she hadn't even confided in her sister how much the failures to date bothered her.

He wasn't sure why she was so at ease with him that she was willing to appeal to him for help—as she'd done when she was looking for a komodo dragon. She'd surprised him with that request. It wasn't every day someone came into his butcher shop and asked for a live giant lizard.

He prided himself on supplying exotic meats for those carnivores in town who liked variety, but he wasn't exactly a specialist in sourcing exotic animals. Not live ones, anyway. That Mellie had come to him for help touched something deep inside.

If he were honest with himself, he'd been attracted to her from almost the first moment they'd met. He'd tried to stay away except for those memorable times when the Alpha had asked him to watch over her safety while Urse was doing her spell work. Peter had tried hard to fight the attraction. He wasn't a good man. He'd seen and done too much in his life to be deserving of a woman as pure of heart and innocent of the world as Mellie.

She was a breath of fresh air in his somewhat jaded existence. She was everything that was good and clean in a world that was too often tainted by dishonesty and deception. He liked her. A lot. Probably too much for her own good, but he was finding it hard to stay away from her.

The self-imposed prohibition on seeking her out had been shattered when she'd come to him, and now, everything seemed to have changed. He couldn't stay away if he tried.

That didn't mean he wanted every nosy bear in the cove to know what was going on. If anything, he was trying to protect her from the inevitable teasing and probing questions. He was taking his cues from her behavior. She hadn't told her sister about the lizard, so Peter extrapolated from that the idea that she didn't want everyone knowing—not even her sister—that she was seeking his help again.

Moreover, Peter didn't really want the whole dragon-blood story going around the cove. The fact that his family line had once held a dragon shifter was a closely held secret in the family. He'd trusted Mellie with the information, but he didn't want everybody to know. Dragon blood had been a curse in the old days. He wasn't sure what it might mean now, but the fact that he'd never run across anyone, in all his travels, who claimed to be a dragon or even to have dragon blood meant that it was probably better to keep such things under his hat. He didn't need anything else to put an even bigger target on his back.

He'd escaped the Soviets with enough of a price on his head. Although it had been many years now, such things didn't just disappear because time passed. That was the reason he had never returned to Mother Russia. He didn't want to stir up trouble for himself, or for what remained of his family who still lived there—particularly his babushka. While she might still be a very scary bear, his grandmother was definitely getting older, and he didn't want to bring trouble to her doorstep.

Speaking of doorsteps… Peter took himself into the bookstore and deliberately let the little bell above the door ring out his presence. It wouldn't do to sneak up on Mellie. She might turn him into a frog or something.

The humorous thought brought a smile to his face as Mellie looked up at him. She was behind the small counter, working on the computer, but she smiled when she saw him.

"Peter," she greeted him warmly. "Thanks for coming. Give me a sec, and I'll close up."

Peter waited while Mellie went over to the door he'd just come in and flipped the sign from OPEN to CLOSED, then locked the deadbolt. He didn't particularly approve of the single lock on the front door, but it wasn't his place to critique security arrangements for the bookstore, no matter how much his inner bear growled at him to do so.

When she returned to him, she invited him into the backroom of the store where the sisters unpacked inventory, kept supplies, and had a private area for any behind-the-scenes work that needed to be done. This was also where the staircase that led up to the apartment above the shop was located.

He followed her upstairs, doing his best not to stare at her butt. It was hard not to focus on the delectable view. Hell, *he* was getting hard, just walking behind her as they went upstairs. This surely must be a form of torture reserved just for him.

Try as he might, Peter couldn't get his mind off her. Kissing her. Licking her all over. Making love with her long into the night.

But it couldn't be. Not now. Not tonight. Maybe never. There was just too much separating them. Years. Life experiences. Magic.

Compared to him, Mellie was almost like a child. Peter had already lived most of a century while Mellie wasn't even thirty yet. He'd left his homeland and participated in wars and conflicts all over the globe. Mellie had left her home in San Francisco for the first time last year when she and her sister had moved to Grizzly Cove, just a few hundred miles up the coast.

He knew all this. Knew how innocent she was in comparison to him. But he'd be damned if he could stop himself from thinking about her in what were probably inappropriate ways, though it didn't feel that way. His brain told him one thing while his heart—and lower regions—told a completely different story.

They entered the apartment, and Peter closed and locked the door to downstairs behind him. It only made sense. He wasn't locking them in together so much as he was locking everyone else—and anything that might somehow threaten her—out. At least, that's what he told himself.

It sure felt like he was locking them together in the tiny space of the apartment, and his inner bear, which usually bristled at confined spaces, was growling happily in his mind. It appeared it liked confined spaces just fine when Mellie was with him. Contrary bear.

"Thanks for agreeing to try this. I honestly don't know what to try next if this doesn't work." Mellie was chatting as she led the way through her apartment toward the front of the building where she'd turned her sister's old room into a potion room, complete with beakers and flasks in all shapes and sizes, along with a portable open-flame grill and various other equipment for her craft.

She had the burner set up near a window, and extra air-handling equipment had been added to help keep the smells down to a minimum, but overall, there was a surprisingly pleasant herbal quality to the air in the room that pleased Peter's sensitive nose. All traces of the earlier disastrous experiments had been wiped away. No acrid scent of burnt grasses and flowers remained from what had happened the night before.

"You cleaned all this last night?" Peter asked, somewhat incredulously.

He'd expected to have to help her get things back in order before they could begin, but that was clearly not the case.

Mellie might sometimes act like the irresponsible younger sister, but she wasn't. In fact, judging by the evidence here, along with things he had noticed when he couldn't help but watch her, she was every bit as industrious and conscientious as her older sister.

"First rule of potion-making: clean up after yourself. You can't brew a pure potion with contaminated materials or vessels. Everything has to be as clean as possible, and blessed in the light of the Goddess's moon, if possible. The new moon can work also—especially when beginning a new task, as I am here. So, last night was a particularly good time to purify everything so I could start fresh."

Peter was impressed. He didn't know all that much about witchcraft, though he didn't hold any prejudices against Mellie's calling. His babushka had occasionally resorted to consulting the *ved'ma* in their village. He remembered that witch fondly. She'd always had kind word for him and occasionally a sweet treat she'd baked in her kitchen. She had also been good friends with his grandmother and was known as a friend to the Clan.

Very few humans had ever been afforded such an honor, so the old magical woman had stood out in his mind. A good memory of an otherwise difficult childhood.

"We're actually lucky Urse married and moved out. She can do her spell work and dream up her chants pretty much anywhere, but a potion *strega* has certain needs for sacred space—or at least space that she can consecrate and keep clean. Urse understood, thankfully, when I asked if we could turn her old room in to a potion chamber. Many siblings would not have been so accommodating." Mellie talked idly as she reached for various components off the shelves she had installed along one wall of the room.

She had jars filled with all kinds of things—most of which, Peter couldn't easily identify just from looking. Most of the jars held dried bits of grasses or flowers, at his best guess. A few held liquids of different colors.

Peter watched as she uncovered something in a large silver

bowl. Immediately, the scent of the mixture in the bowl reached his nostrils. It was a potent combination of different herbs and other substances. He peered over her shoulder and realized that everything had been pulverized so that the contents of the bowl was a sort of gritty paste.

"I prepped the base of the potion last night so we don't have too much more to do here. Just add a few wet ingredients and then see if your blood is enough to kick-start the magic," she told him, placing the bowl on the workbench situated in front of the window.

He noted a cut crystal pitcher filled with sparkling water also waited on the countertop. There was a mortar and pestle, along with a few sprigs of what smelled like fresh cut pine twigs with needles. Several different varieties he recognized from the woods around the cove.

"I collected these last night. The idea is to unite the water and the land in solidarity against evil." She turned toward the window, which faced the setting sun over the waters of the cove, and held each twig aloft, murmuring a prayer before she took three needles from each kind of twig she'd collected and put them in the bowl of her mortar and pestle set. She then began grinding them into a paste as she spoke blessings over them.

Peter wasn't sure what he was supposed to do, so he just stood quietly and watched, adding his own silent prayers that this would work. He'd hate to see disappointment on her face again. He wasn't all that confident that his blood would do anything special—his connection to his dragon ancestor was thin, at best—but he wanted Mellie to be happy. This potion thing was putting a lot of stress on her and had stolen the joy from the young woman who'd been so carefree and jovial just a few months before.

He wanted Mellie to be that way again. He'd do anything in his power to help that come about. It was his mission. Inside, his bear agreed with that thought, adding the beast's sense of approval for his human half's plans.

CHAPTER THREE

Mellie felt a bit self-conscious, knowing Peter was watching her every move. It was also oddly comforting, in a way, to not be all alone while she was brewing her potion. Before Urse had married John, Mellie always knew her sister was around if Mel needed help or advice. Even if Urse wasn't in the room when Mellie was brewing a potion, she was a presence—a highly magical presence—in her life, available and nearby should Mel need her.

Now that Urse had moved out and gone to live with her mate in his den, that had changed. Even though she wasn't very far away as the crow flies, the feeling of Urse in the apartment was gone. She wouldn't just pop in and remind Mel to stop and eat dinner or ask if she needed anything. Theoretically, she *could* still do that, but Urse was so wrapped up in being a newlywed that it hadn't happened since Urse had moved out.

Mellie was a little lonely, if she was honest. Peter was good company. He wasn't overly chatty, though he was a bit more talkative than some of the other guys in town. Mellie loved the timbre of his lightly accented voice and could listen to him for hours, if he'd let her. She didn't have any plans to tell him that, though.

She sent her prayers up to the Goddess as she worked, Peter standing companionably beside her. He was both a distraction and a comfort. Overall, it was nice to have him here, even if she had to keep dragging her mind back to the matter at hand.

"Would you pour half the carafe of water into the silver bowl, please?" she asked, hoping to get him involved in the work and get her mind back on business at the same time.

"Are you sure my wild bear energy won't mess with your spell?"

She took him seriously for a short moment before catching the glint of humor in his dark eyes.

"It's the dragon part I'm interested in tonight, but no, simply pouring water into the base potion won't require any magic on your part." She turned back to her work and heard water splashing gently into the silver bowl next to her. Peter was a warm presence at her side. Closer now that she'd given him a task.

When he put the crystal carafe back on the table, she reached for it. "I think this is nearly done." She poured a few drops of water in to the bowl and then poured the resulting green mixture into the silver vessel, closing her eyes at the last to speak words of high magic.

When she opened her eyes again, the dark green and brown liquid in the silver chalice was beginning to bubble. Timing was critical.

She turned to Peter. "I have purified my athame and sterilized it, as well," she told him, gesturing toward the silver dagger on the countertop. "It is a sacred blade, and I offer it to you, for use in tonight's work. Or, you could use your own blade. It's your choice."

"Would the potion be stronger if we used your special knife?" he asked her.

She raised one shoulder in a half-shrug. "There are benefits to either approach. Your own blade should already carry your magic and intentions. My blade is consecrated and as clean of other influences as I can make it right now. Honestly, either will work, though I'm beginning to believe that free will has a lot to do with the success of this potion."

"Whose free will?"

"Yours. Or the dragon's," she corrected herself. "Since you're my dragon stand-in, yours. In fact, I'd like you to do the honors, so there can be no question that your blood is freely given. Using your own knife would only reinforce that idea, I think."

"How much blood are we talking about?"

His brows drew together, making her want to reach up and stroke his forehead until he relaxed again. It was a silly, stray thought that heightened her awareness of him and her reaction to his presence.

"Three drops," she answered, trying to keep her mind on the business at hand. He was making it tough, though. The sexy beast.

His wrinkled brow smoothed all on its own. "That's all? I thought you would need more." His accent worked its magic on her spine, making her warm from within, though she did her best to hide her reaction.

This always happened whenever she talked to him for any length of time. She was surprised she hadn't melted into a puddle at his feet already, but apparently, she hid her arousal well enough that he didn't notice…or pretended not to.

To distract herself, she went to the bookshelf and took down the book her grandmother had recently acquired at great personal magical cost. Nonna had bartered some of her magical workings for use of this ancient grimoire. She wouldn't tell Mellie or Urse exactly what the mage who was now the official caretaker of this book had required of Nonna, but it had to be something complex. Nonna was both clairvoyant and a very powerful *strega* in her own right, and she had friends all over the magical community. One of whom had loaned them this book…for a price.

"Is that the book?" Peter asked, his tone full of curiosity.

"The ancient Grimoire of Andalusia," Mellie breathed respectfully as she stroked the cover of the ancient book. "After the Phoenicians came the Carthaginians. But, when Hannibal tried to fight off the Romans, he failed, and the region became known for a time as Baetica, part of the Roman Empire. It was the birthplace of the Emperor Trajan and probably Hadrian, as well. It was during the time of Rome in Andalusia that the first *strega* of the area began writing this book. Her descendants added to it down through the centuries until it became the powerful repository of arcane knowledge it is today." She walked carefully to the work bench and put the book into a cradle Mellie had prepared for it.

Mellie lit a white candle and gently opened the book. The pages moved as Mellie held her hands over the book, opening to the recipe she needed. It was the only thing the grimoire would show her, and it was the answer to the question she'd put to the book time and time again. Somehow, this potion was what she needed, but finding the right ingredients had been a task of monumental proportions. She had everything now…except the dragon's blood. Hopefully, Peter would be a good enough substitute to make the potion work this time.

"What happened to the *strega* in that region after the fall of the Roman Empire?" Peter asked as Mellie moved back from the book that would give up no more of its secrets than that which she had already seen.

Mellie looked at him and thought back. "The Vandals came through, then the Visigoths, then the Eastern Roman Emperor Justinian I called it Spania in the sixth century A.D. as part of the Byzantine Empire. Then, the followers of Mohammad came in the eighth century and called it Al-Andalus. In the tenth century, the followers of Christ were fighting back, and by the thirteenth century, most of the land had gone back to Christian rule. But it wasn't until the fall of Grenada in 1492—the same year Christopher Columbus set sail for the New World—that the last bit of the Iberian Peninsula was united under the Kingdom of Castile. Then, of course, evil ran over the land in the 1500's. Drought and famine. Plague and pestilence. All hallmarks of the Destroyer and her followers. But the *strega* of Andalusia survived it all and kept working on the book. Adding knowledge with each generation. There was more strife in the 1800's with Napoleon's shenanigans, but the area remains part of Spain. Who knows what the next few centuries will bring?"

"I didn't realize you were such a student of history," Peter said respectfully.

Mellie flushed a little, realizing that she'd given him a bit more than he'd probably wanted. "Sorry. When the book came to me, I made it my business to brush up on its history. Plus, I should warn you, I was a history major in college. I enjoy studying the past. Always have."

"You must have learned a lot from the book," he offered, gesturing toward the ancient tome on the stand.

"You'd think so, but it only shows the reader what they need at the time. I need a potion recipe to push back the leviathan and its minions, so that's all it's been showing me." She shrugged as she checked on the base stock for the potion, which was bubbling nicely now. "I'm almost ready to try this, if you are. Just a minute or two more for it to get to full strength."

"I promised to help you, and I will." Peter bent slightly to retrieve the knife he apparently kept in a sheath in his boot. Mellie looked at the gleaming blade. He kept it in good order, which boded well for the spell. "How did the book get that way? Does it have magic of its own?"

"Only the magic that the *strega* who wrote in it passed to it through the centuries. Many protective spells. Many spells that aim to prevent its misuse. Layer upon layer of protections, each with the particular flavor of the witch who placed them. Some were potion masters, like me. Some were spell casters, like Urse. Some had other powers and ways to realize them. All of that magic is both chronicled in the book and was used to protect it."

She gazed fondly at the book. Her family had one like it,

but it remained in Nonna's sister's possession, back in the old country. Nonna had tried to get use of that one first, but it had not contained a spell that could help in this case. It had been Nonna's sister who had arranged for the use of the Andalusian book through her contacts.

Mellie checked the brew again and judged it ready. "Okay. It's show time. Come over here, and let's do this, and we'll see if it works."

Peter moved right up next to her, holding the tip of his knife to one of his fingers. Oddly, he'd chosen the ring finger on his left hand even before she opened her mouth to instruct him to do so. How had he known she'd suggest the finger that was thought to connect with the heart?

Or had it just been an arbitrary choice on his part? No time to ask now. There was work to do.

"Just a little prick of the finger, and three drops of blood is all we need. Not fast. Spaced apart. I'll be chanting invocations before and after each drop, so give me time to utter the words, okay?" She looked up at him, glad to see he was taking this as seriously as she was.

"Just give me the signal," he told her. "I'll follow your lead."

She paused a moment before proceeding, tilting her head and considering him. A hint of humor flashed through her. She couldn't help it. Being around Peter always made her feel joyful deep down inside.

"Think dragony thoughts," she told him, offering a quick smile.

He chuckled at her words, and the tension level in the room lowered a notch. Good. Magic was always better done when things were calm and spirits were in a happy place.

She checked the base potion again. "I think we're ready to go. I'll nod each time it's your turn to do your thing."

He nodded his own agreement, and she began the ritual. Her words invoked the Goddess and all the forces of Light in this realm and beyond. There was a sanctity to the ancient words, and she spoke them in the old tongue. Most ancient *strega* recipes and chants were written and spoken in Latin, and that nearly forgotten language had been a requirement in her schooling that had come in very handy as she worked with old manuscripts.

It was especially important in light of the fact that Nonna had foretold that it would be Mellie who would become the next Ricoletti *strega* to add pages to the family grimoire. That would have to be done in Latin, as well, and Mellie took her grandmother's prediction seriously. Nonna's gift of foresight was never something to take lightly.

Mellie came to the end of her opening lines and nodded to Peter. He did not hesitate but used the sharp tip of his blade to pierce the skin of his fingertip and allowed a single drop of his blood to land in the middle of the silver bowl.

The effect was immediate as the potion changed color and began to bubble more fiercely. What had been a muddy green-brown was now a startling, shiny teal color. This hadn't happened before. This was a good sign. Mellie allowed her hopes to rise, but the next two drops would tell the tale. She began reciting her lines again, the Latin words tripping off her tongue.

Finishing the next piece quickly, she nodded again to Peter. He tilted his finger and allowed a second drop to fall into the chalice. The color changed again. This time, it went to a shocking lime green, glistening the way she imagined a dragon's scales might shine in the sun. The bubbling continued to increase, though no vapor came off the concoction. That was the final test. If the potion could manifest the dragon's breath—basically a small amount of white smoky fog that remained even when the potion was still—then she would have succeeded. At least, that's what the book said.

Mellie went into the next set of ancient words and then nodded to Peter one last time. He tipped his finger and the last drop of blood dropped into the silver cauldron. The color flashed, and Mellie had to blink as the reaction completed. Quickly, she recited the last invocation and waved her hands over the silver bowl, hoping for at least a wisp of fog.

A tiny stream of white rose…and then subsided back into the potion. So close!

The color of the concoction was a healthy green now. The green of forests and trees. Evergreen. Like the landscape all around the cove, now almost overrun by bear shifters. Mellie wasn't a hundred percent sure, but she suspected the potion would have been a different color had the dragon side of Peter's lineage been stronger. As it was, they'd managed to brew a potion that wasn't a complete failure. It hadn't exploded or otherwise destroyed itself, for one thing.

For another, it held a pure magic of its own. Not exactly what she'd intended, but not something bad either. Peter's bear side had won the day, but the bear was plenty strong itself. This potion was a protective one, and it appeared stable. Mellie would bottle it and test it to see how strong its protective properties were. She couldn't be altogether sure, but she suspected it was a slightly weaker version of what she'd been aiming for.

"I'm sorry," Peter said, peering over her shoulder at the potion. "I have the impression that's not what you wanted."

"It's not bad," she told him, studying the potion and gauging its magic as best she could from merely looking at it. "Maybe not quite what the book promised, but I think that's more because you're mostly bear and the presence of dragon in your blood wasn't as strong as the potion requires. Still, this is a powerful protective elixir. It will not go to waste, and your sacrifice will be used to help protect the people of this town. I promise you that."

She turned to him, finding him much closer than she expected. Suddenly, her breath caught in her throat. He was standing so close, all she had to do was reach up on tiptoes… And then… She was kissing him.

Or, perhaps he was kissing her. It didn't really matter who had initiated it, though she privately thought maybe they'd both reached for each other at the same time. All she knew was that it was wonderful to finally be kissing the man who had been at the center of her daydreams for months now.

His arms were tight around her, and his kiss sent her senses into orbit. Peter was just the right combination of strong and gentle, power wrapped in velvet, desire tempered by care.

She felt all that from his kiss, and her spirit soaked it in, wonder filling her at the feeling of being cared for by this amazing man. How could a simple kiss impart so much feeling? She wasn't sure, but she had no doubt what her senses were telling her was true.

In some way, Peter cared for her. His kiss told her all of that and more. It hinted at the desire that she knew now was shared. She'd wanted to experience his kiss—and a whole lot more—for so long now. She felt that same yearning in him.

Maybe she was reading his magical aura. She'd been able to do that on occasion, and with her hands on his body, she'd never been closer to him physically.

She wasn't just touching his aura, she was standing within it. Enveloped by the core strength of a man she'd come to respect and desire above all others. It was a novel experience, and incredibly arousing.

His magical energy meshed with hers beautifully. There was no moment of resistance. No fear that they would be incompatible.

No, with Peter, all was ease and simplicity. The attraction of opposites and the smooth blending of their energies to create something bigger and even more intense. The magic fueled her desire, and she took the kiss deeper, lifting her leg to wrap around his hip.

Peter seemed to understand her silent pleading, lifting her up with his hands under her butt cheeks and carrying her to a clear spot on the countertop. He placed her on the edge, stepping between her thighs and dragging her closer to the object of her desire.

The ridge of his cock rubbed up against the seam of her pants, and she wanted to curse the fabric that separated them. She pushed at his shoulders, hoping he would remove his shirt, but he didn't comply. Needy, she moaned, and the sound seemed to stop him in his tracks.

Peter pulled back and looked into her eyes, both of them breathing hard. "This is too fast," he told her, his accent thicker in passion, which made her body tingle even more.

"No," she told him, unable to speak coherently at the moment.

Peter shook his head, his hair disheveled from her fingers running through it. She loved the look on him. She wanted to mess up his hair some more.

He rested his forehead against hers. "You are too important to me to do this too quickly," he told her, making her breath catch as the seriousness in his tone.

What was he saying? Was he implying…?

Peter stepped back, making sure she was seated firmly on the countertop first before he separated them. She wanted to go after him, but her mind was captured by the words he'd spoken—and the ones he hadn't. Intrigued didn't begin to cover how she was feeling.

A million questions raced through her mind, but she didn't have the courage to voice even one. She didn't want to be wrong and embarrass herself, possibly wrecking their friendship forever.

Though, it really sounded like he wanted to take their relationship beyond friendship. *Well* beyond, if she was a very lucky girl.

"I'm really sorry, Mel," he repeated as he moved away.

"Don't be sorry," she whispered, not wanting him to leave thinking she hadn't been an equal part of that scorching kiss. She had to be bold or she might lose him to misunderstanding. She dragged her tiny bits of courage together and tried to sound braver than she was. "I've wanted to kiss you for a while now."

He stopped moving away and met her gaze, one of his eyebrows rising in question, his eyes dancing with…something. Joy? Amusement? Desire?

"You have?" he asked as she remembered to be bold and

held his gaze, even as her blood began to tingle all throughout her body.

Peter had the most amazing effect on her. Truth to tell, he always had. From the first moment they'd met.

She nodded, unable to speak.

Peter started to move toward her again, his gaze holding hers with clear intent. Oh, boy. She was going to get it now. Yay!

Then, the phone rang. She could clearly hear it ringing in the main room of the apartment. There was an extension in her bedroom, too, but none in the potion room. She'd done that on purpose. Only, now, it was a total pain in the butt.

Peter stilled, and the intent look in his eyes dulled a bit. "Are you expecting a call?"

"No," she told him, already sliding off the counter top. "It's probably my sister checking up on me, and if I don't answer, she'll be here in no time flat." Mellie loved her sister, but right at this moment, she could happily wish her into another country. "I'm sorry," she told Peter, pausing as she passed him to lay one hand on his shoulder. His warm, muscular shoulder.

Damn. She wanted to scream at Urse for interrupting just when things were getting interesting, but she couldn't even do that because Urse didn't know Peter was here. Double damn.

"Hello?" Mellie snatched up the telephone, miffed that her interlude with Peter had been interrupted.

"Is that any way to greet your nonna?" came the unexpected voice over the phone.

"Nonna! I thought it was Urse, checking up on me."

The old woman sighed. "Sometimes, I wish you had just a touch of my gift, so you'd know what was coming next. You and your bear did good work tonight, but it wasn't enough."

"Nonna," she repeated, a bit shocked, even though she'd grown up with her grandmother's flashes of insight.

It wasn't an all-the-time thing. Nonna saw visions of important stuff, but it wasn't reliable. Sometimes, the visions didn't come for months at a time. Sometimes, they came in rapid succession. Nobody could say when or why as far as Mellie understood.

"Don't sound so surprised. I was young once, too," Nonna reminded her granddaughter. "Your bear has a pure soul, though his past is quite colorful."

"What did you do? Have him investigated?" Mellie whispered into the phone in a scandalized tone.

"Bah," Nonna made a mildly disgusted sound. "That Collin Hastings wouldn't take my money. Said he refused to rat on one of his own. Whether he meant a fellow shifter or that your bear was a personal friend or colleague, I'm not sure. The only thing he would tell me was just what I said. That your Peter's past was quite colorful."

"I can't believe you called the shifter private eye!" Mellie was totally scandalized now.

Everyone in their magical circles was aware of the specialized services Hastings provided to the supernatural community, though he worked mostly for his own kind—shifters of all species. He, himself, was able to shift into some kind of bird of prey, or so the rumors went.

"Like I said, he wouldn't take the case. Cagey fellow, for a bird shifter." Nonna made a dismissive sound then cleared her throat. "But, for now, you get your mind back on business, young lady. Tell that bear to go home and let you do your work. No distractions."

Nonna tried to sound stern, but Mellie heard the humor in her tone. Nonna was like that—a big softie, even when trying to be a disciplinarian.

"Tell her I'm going," came Peter's deep voice from just behind Mellie's shoulder, making her jump. Mellie put the phone away from her ear, pressing it to her shoulder.

"Did you hear all of that?" She cringed, hoping he wouldn't be offended by her grandmother's nosiness.

Peter nodded. "Shifter hearing is pretty good, you know. And it's all right. Collin called yesterday and told me a little old Italian lady from San Francisco had been asking about me. I wasn't offended. It's clear she is doing her best to protect you, even long-distance." Peter's eyes held laughter, not anger, for which Mellie was truly grateful.

"I'm *so* sorry." Her cheeks flushed with embarrassment.

"Don't be. She loves you." He shrugged, smiling. "I'm leaving now. Lock the door behind me and tell your nonna I said hello."

He paused slightly, dipping his head to kiss her on the forehead. Not exactly the goodnight kiss she was hoping for, but she'd take it. The gesture felt intimate. Special.

Then, he was gone, and Mellie was left with her grandmother on the phone for company.

Peter's bear refused to settle. Those spectacular kisses with Mellie were even better than he'd imagined they'd be. Now that he'd had a taste of her, he wanted more. Much more. But there were still valid reasons why anything between them might be…inadvisable, at best.

For one thing, what would his grandmother say? Babushka was on her way here, though he wasn't sure exactly when she would arrive. She was a very independent bear. If she wanted to take the scenic route from Mother Russia to the good ol' USA, Peter could not gainsay her.

At least, it wouldn't be wise—or all that safe—to do so. Babushka was still a mighty bear, even if she was getting older.

He didn't know how she was going to take the news that the only woman his bear had ever pushed him toward mating was a witch. Not just a witch, but an Italian *strega*, who came from a long line of powerful *strega* before her.

Peter stopped short at his own thoughts as he walked down the Main Street of Grizzly Cove, heading for the stretch of woods that led to his cabin. Was he really thinking *mate* when it came to Mellie?

He tested that thought out. Rolled it around in his mind and savored it for a while…

Yep. He was definitely thinking mate. Wow.

Goddess help them both.

CHAPTER FOUR

With his inner bear still unable to settle after the revelations of the evening, Peter sought the solace of the woods around his den. He'd deliberately built his home into the side of the mountain that formed one edge of the cove. He'd dug his log cabin into the side of the hill, extending the construction back into the earth itself. The front of the house made it look like a small log cabin, but it was really rather large inside.

It was surrounded by pristine forest. There were even a few super tall redwood trees that stood silent sentinel on the land he had claimed as his own territory. He felt as if he had been given guardianship over a sacred place, and that the trees—many of which were much older than he was—were watching over his home and keeping their barky eye on him, so to speak.

He'd carefully chosen deadfall logs to build his home. He hadn't taken the life of any living tree. It might seem odd to the other men, but it was a little quirk of Peter's that the shaman seemed to understand. At least one bear didn't think he was crazy for the way he'd chosen to build his place. Gus wasn't exactly the run-of-the-mill bear shifter either, though.

No, he was a rare spirit bear. His cream-colored coat stood out in the dark forest as Peter roamed the perimeter of his territory in bear form. It was as if the spirit bear—his buddy Gus—was waiting for him.

Peter approached cautiously, and they walked in parallel for a while, stalking silently through the woods in harmony for the moment. Gus's presence had a calming effect on Peter's riled nerves. The spirit bear was a holy man. A shaman. A priest of sorts. He was good to be around, and Peter found himself wondering if Gus had somehow known that Peter needed his soothing influence that night.

Peter wouldn't put it past his friend to know the unknowable—including Peter's odd mood. Whether or not Gus would know what caused it was another matter. Mellie's grandmother might be clairvoyant, but as far as Peter knew, his friend Gus didn't lean that way. At least, he thought not.

Eventually, they worked their way around the perimeter of Peter's territory and ended up back at the cabin. Peter shifted as he walked toward the front door, hoping Gus would follow. He needed someone he trusted to talk to, and Gus was just about the most trustworthy bear of Peter's acquaintance. Of course, Peter would trust—and had trusted—each of the members of the old team with his life, but emotions were tricky. Talking about them was even harder for a guy like him. Talking with Gus was easier than talking to any of the other guys about stuff like that, though, because Gus had that whole mystical thing going on. The spirit bear was downright spooky.

Peter threw on the jeans he'd left behind when he'd gone furry and headed for the kitchen. He was always a little hungry after going bear. He looked through his refrigerator and pulled out a plate of venison steaks. Yeah, that would hit the spot.

"How many of these you want?" he asked Gus, who was dressed in a pair of sweatpants Peter had last seen lying on top of the stack of folded laundry he had yet to put away.

Peter didn't mind. Clothing was shared freely after a shift

because they were all trying to fly under the radar, posing as a human community. That meant clothing. Which wasn't always readily available after a shift, but necessary in order to maintain the illusion of normalcy, so one took what one could find, and nobody complained. The custom was to return anything you borrowed, freshly laundered, in a reasonable amount of time. So far, the system was working well.

"Can you spare three? I skipped a meal or two today," Gus said, taking a seat at the kitchen island on a high stool.

Peter had installed a full chef's kitchen, complete with a grill right there in the cabin. He might be a hearty Russian bear, but that didn't mean he enjoyed grilling outside in the winter.

"No problem," Peter assured the other man. "There's more where these came from."

"Handy being the town butcher," Gus agreed.

Peter kept busy over the next half hour or more, preparing the impromptu meal. They ate in companionable silence, concentrating on their hunger and their food for the first few minutes after the meal was served.

After the immediate hunger was sated, Peter felt much calmer than he had earlier in the day. Gus was a good friend. He knew when to talk and when to hold his counsel until Peter was ready to hear it.

"I believe I may have found my mate," Peter said, surprising himself at his own candor.

He hadn't meant to blurt anything out, much less the deepest thoughts in his mind, but Gus didn't even blink. Instead, Gus chewed, narrowing his eyes thoughtfully on his fork, not looking directly at Peter.

"Matters of the heart can be very unsettling," Gus said quietly. "More so when the mind is not in harmony with the soul."

"You think I lack harmony?" Peter scoffed, though he sensed truth in the spirit bear's words.

"Your mind is troubled. You bear is confused. Why is

that?" Finally, Gus looked at Peter, spearing him with his dark eyes.

Peter sighed heavily. "It's Mellie." Just saying her name made his heart leap, and his thoughts fill with the shadows of doubt.

"The *strega*?" Now Gus frowned. "I think I understand. To mate a woman of power can be a difficult path, but it is one worth pursuing if she truly is your mate."

"My bear thinks she is, but there are many obstacles to overcome." Peter felt the scowl on his own face but was powerless to calm his thoughts or his features.

"Are these true obstacles or problems of your own making?" Gus wanted to know.

"Can a witch of such power mate truly with one of us?" Peter wondered aloud.

"Just look at John and Urse," Gus answered immediately. "If you have doubt, I can tell you from my perspective, theirs is a true mating that will last as long as they do."

That was actually very reassuring. John and Urse seemed so perfect together, but they were still in the early part of their relationship…the honeymoon phase. If anyone would know whether or not the match was a true mating, it would be the spirit bear. True mates never parted and recognized each other quickly—at least among shifters. Peter wasn't entirely sure how it worked when one half of the pair was a shifter, but the other was a powerful mage.

"What will our families make of each other? The Ricolettis may be welcoming toward a bear shifter, but I have doubts my babushka or my extended family will be as accepting of a *strega*." Peter frowned harder. His family could be very stubborn, and although he didn't see them as often as he once did, they were still close.

"Your grandmother is on her way here, isn't she?" Gus asked.

Peter nodded. "She could be here any day now."

"Then, I suppose you will have your answer soon. I have no doubt your granny will not mince words when she sees which way the wind is blowing. For now, I suggest you just go with the flow. Enjoy your time with Mellie and continue to explore your growing feelings. If she is the one for you, even your babushka cannot stand in your way, when it comes right down to it. Mating is sacred. If Mellie is your true mate, we will all accept the bond. And, if your family does not, then you know you have another family here among the bears of Grizzly Cove."

Gus clapped Peter on the shoulder, and the two men shared a moment of silent acceptance. Gus was good like that. He made Peter remember the bonds of comradeship that bound him so tightly to the men he had worked with for so many years and now shared this social experiment of a town with. The men of their old unit, who had founded Grizzly Cove, were his brothers. If his blood family rejected his choices, he knew he would always find acceptance among his chosen family here in the cove.

*

Mellie didn't really want an audience for her casting, but she needed input from the mer on the effect of the potion she and Peter had managed to brew the night before. For some reason, Peter had brought his friend Gus along, too. Mellie knew Gus was supposed to be some sort of shaman to the local Native American tribe that made its home just to the south of the cove, but Mellie hadn't had much contact with the man and didn't know him well. Still, if Peter valued his opinion, Mellie was willing to give the man the benefit of the doubt.

So, it was a strange little group that met down by the shoreline, just inside the mouth of the cove. They were at the point where Urse's ward held creatures of evil at bay, unable to enter the waters of the cove itself. Mellie had chosen to try her potion from a position that would minimize her possible exposure. She'd have to get right down to the water to put her potion in while speaking the ritual words. The currents would carry the potion and its magic where they willed, hopefully casting a wider barrier that evil could not cross.

At least, that was the theory.

Mellie wasn't really sure what would happen in practice. Possibly, nothing. Hopefully, something. Whatever happened, they'd at least know if Mellie was on the right track with this preparation. It had been so long, and she had so little to show for her efforts. This was the first time she'd actually had something worth trying, and she was going to make the most of this opportunity.

Accordingly, she'd asked for help from the mer. She wanted someone with magical sensing abilities in the water, able to report back to Mellie where her potion went and what effects it had. They were doing this at high noon, when the sun was brightest overhead so visibility would be at its zenith, as well. If all went well.

At least the sun was out today. So far, so good.

Mellie had chosen the point of the cove where a circle of young standing stones stood sentinel. When Peter had heard her intended destination, he'd immediately called his friend Gus. Mellie was vaguely aware that Gus was the caretaker of the sacred circle, and if the ring wasn't on his land, per se, it was very, very close. She wasn't sure, exactly.

Regardless, it was probably for that reason that Peter had wanted the resident bear around to watch the proceedings. Mellie didn't mind. She already had a mer audience. Her request for help had netted her several mer helpers to watch along the barrier of Urse's ward and report back their findings. She would've been happy with just one observer, but it looked like they'd given her a whole platoon.

Which would make this all that much more embarrassing if the potion fizzled as soon as it hit the water. Mellie sent a silent prayer up, hoping this wasn't going to be a complete failure. She had already warned everyone that this was only a trial run. She'd explained that she was missing one key ingredient to her potion but had been able to brew a weaker version by making a substitution. She'd done all she could to not get everyone's hopes up that her first attempt was going to be as big a success as her sister's spell work.

Urse had created some pretty big shoes to fill. Her spells had been perfection from day one. She'd done a series of four spells on four successive days, each one building on the previous until she'd been able to ward the entire cove. It had been a master work. A feat Urse had never achieved before and might never do again in her entire life.

And it had set the bar really high for Mellie. Too high, perhaps, though Mellie would do her best to meet or exceed her sister's work. Not for any competitive reason, but because the people of Grizzly Cove needed protection. They deserved the best Mellie could give, and then some. She wanted to do it for them. For her new home. For her new people.

She loved this town and had quickly decided it was home. She might've grown up in San Francisco, and heaven knew, she missed her nonna, who still lived there, but Grizzly Cove felt like the place she's always been meant to be.

Mellie didn't say anything to Gus or even Peter as she went about her business. It was enough that they were there, in the background, to witness whatever would happen with this potion. She hoped it would at least do *something*. It might not be the exact right formulation yet, but if this potion worked even just a little, it would be the first positive step forward she'd had since embarking on this quest.

Deciding to just concentrate on doing the best job she possibly could as she cast her spell via her potion, Mellie set to work. She sent up prayers to the Mother of All, sanctifying the space around her as she worked. She would launch the potion from just behind the barrier of the ward for safety reasons. There was no sense getting too close to the unprotected area of shore before she was certain her potion was going to really work. For this test, safety was the better part of valor.

Not that the evil creatures weren't watching her every move. She could see the tentacles rising occasionally out of the water in a menacing display. She could feel the oppressive anger of their evil, as well, and it wasn't a good feeling. Best to get on with her work.

When all was ready, she looked out to the water, seeing the head of the closest mermaid pop above the gentle waves. Mellie gave the prearranged thumbs-up signal that meant she was about to start her test. Then, Mellie looked back at Peter and Gus.

"Stand back. I'm about to give this a whirl," she warned them, not waiting for a response before turning back to her work.

Gathering herself and taking a deep breath, she grounded her energy and centered her focus. Then, with pure intent and a chant of prayer to the Goddess, Mellie walked slowly to the water and emptied the vial of her new potion into the lapping wavelets just at the shoreline.

When the vial was empty, Mellie retreated from the shore, walking backwards and keeping her eyes on the water. It wouldn't do to give the enemy her back for even the shortest moment. Even if she thought she was safe behind the ward. Evil was canny. She had to be cautious.

The mermaid dove under the water, and Mellie tried to follow the progress of her potion out into the water. She thought she saw the moment when the first hints of the new magic crossed the barrier of Urse's ward. The reaction of the closest of the leviathan's minions let her know that something was causing them trouble. Mellie almost smiled, but she didn't like to see any living creature in pain—even an evil one.

Still, if the creature would only retreat, the pain would cease. That's what the potion was all about. It was meant to drive the evil creatures back, away from the shore. It wasn't intended to kill them. According to Nonna and others, such things could not be killed in the mortal realm because they were creatures who were forever tied to the forgotten realm from which they had been conjured. The best that Mellie could hope for was to protect the shore and the waters a short distance out so that mortals and mer alike could go about the business of living in safety. It would be up to a different kind of magic than her own to banish the leviathan and its minions back to its native realm.

"Looks like it's doing something." Peter's voice sounded at her side. She glanced over to find him watching the water, as she had been. Gus was next to him, doing the same.

"It appears to be pushing the smaller creatures back," Gus put in. "And the ward is holding, not that there was much doubt about that."

Of course not, Mellie thought carefully to herself. Urse was a *real* witch. One of the most talented of their generation—or so Nonna said. She'd always included Mellie in the praise, but Mel was beginning to think she'd done so only out of kindness. Urse had proven her skills. She'd warded an entire town and part of the coast with permanent wards. That wasn't something just anyone could do. Permanent wards were rare. So rare, not even one witch in every generation could cast them. It was more like one witch in ten generations. And they usually cost the mage greatly in personal power to cast them, so it wasn't something ever done lightly.

There were few permanent wards in existence in the world today, even though mages had been trying to cast them for eons. Urse's wards would stand the test of time. They would be there long after she and her sister were merely memories. The ability to cast permanent wards was sort of Urse's superpower.

Mellie had always been told she had a destiny as bright as her sister's, but she was seriously doubting herself and her supposed power at this point. Mellie wasn't used to failure on this scale. Sure, she'd made the usual mistakes young witches make as they learn their craft, but she hadn't messed up this badly—over and over again during the past few months—since she was a kid.

"It's having a real effect," Gus said at her shoulder. He'd moved closer without her being aware of it. Bears were stealthy, so she'd gotten used to people sneaking up on her since moving here. Gus pointed, and Mellie followed the direction of his lifted arm. "Even the larger ones are scattering now."

Sure enough, Mellie could see that among the flailing tentacles, some were of a much larger size now. The little ones had scattered first, but as the potion wove its way out into the ocean, the larger minions were fleeing from it too. Mellie felt a sense of accomplishment. This might not be the permanent solution she was seeking just yet, but it was certainly a big step forward.

"I may not be much of a dragon, but the bear blood is strong," Peter commented with a bit of smug satisfaction in his tone. Mellie figured he was entitled.

"Yes, it is," she agreed with him, turning to give him a smile. He was looking at her, too, and their eyes met…and held. Time stood still as they shared a moment.

"Wait," Gus said, recalling them both to the present. "Here comes the big guy." His tone was ominous.

Mellie looked out in time to see the behemoth of sea monsters approaching. It was near enough to the surface that they could make out the top of its massive tentacles. This was the leviathan itself. It had already tried and failed to cross Urse's ward many times, according to the mer who patrolled the ward every moment of the day and night. Its smaller minions were fleeing away from Mellie's potion, but the big guy…

Damn. The big guy was sailing right through as if nothing much had happened. Mellie's spirits fell. It didn't look like her newest potion had any effect at all on the biggest problem they faced. The leviathan was just too strong.

CHAPTER FIVE

Peter escorted Mellie back to town. Gus had opted to stay behind to observe the potion's effects more closely. He was watching, in particular, to see if the effect dissipated and the smaller minions were able to return closer to the ward. For all they knew, the effect might've been just a temporary thing.

Peter hadn't voiced that concern where Mellie could hear. She was down in the dumps enough already. He hated seeing her so miserable and wished there was something he could do to raise her spirits. He just didn't know what.

When they arrived back at the bookstore, Urse was waiting for them. She instructed them to head directly over to the mayor's office where her mate, John, was waiting for them along with Nansee, the leader of the mer pod that now lived in the cove. They'd received early reports from the scouts along the ward on the potion's effect in the water, and John wanted to talk to Mellie about it.

Peter went with her. He wouldn't be separated from her when she had to face the Alpha bear in his den. Office. Whatever. John's inner sanctum at town hall might as well be his secondary den. He spent enough time there running the town.

Peter was glad he'd decided to stick with Mellie, because when they got to town hall, it wasn't just John and Nansee waiting for her. No, there was a full-fledged council meeting happening in the big conference room. Peter would have been invited anyway, since he was part of the core group that had founded the town and therefore on the council, but even he had to admit, facing down a room full of bear shifters had to be a little intimidating for a petite human mage like Mellie.

She walked in, her spine straight, her chin lifted as if daring the bears to criticize her recent performance. He knew she wasn't happy with the results. He knew she was having doubts about her own power, but she didn't let it show to this room full of predators. Good girl. She was as smart and courageous as she was beautiful.

Peter stayed right at her side, growling at the bear shifter who was sitting next to the seat they'd left open for Mellie until the other man moved to Peter's seat across the room. Peter was going to stand at Mellie's side no matter what.

"First, let me thank you on behalf of the entire town for the work you've put in on this project, Amelia," John said formally, opening the meeting. "Urse told me how conscientious you've been and how difficult your task."

Peter was pleased with the way the Alpha bear talked to Mellie. John was a good leader and knew how to motivate people and make them feel their worth. It was why he'd followed John as his Alpha for so long.

"Now, let's hear from the mer leader," John proposed. "Then, perhaps Peter will be kind enough to provide observations from land."

Peter nodded in accord with John's plan for the meeting and deferred to Nansee, who sat next to John. The mer leader and the bear Alpha had developed what looked like a good working relationship, especially since Nansee and Urse had become close friends.

Peter wondered how Mellie got along with the mer leader. Urse had status as John's mate. She was Alpha female, for lack of a better term, and Nansee and she were about equal in rank, though, of course, the land-based shifters took precedence in the town. Nansee was still in charge of her pod, even while they were on land, but they came under the Alpha bear's protection here, and he was considered the higher power here in town, while Nansee still ruled under the water. So far, the arrangement had worked out well, mostly because the two leaders were willing to work together and Nansee was able to defer to the Alpha bear who had offered her and her pod sanctuary in the cove when the leviathan had threatened them.

Still, Mellie's place in the hierarchy wasn't entirely clear. She was sister to the Alpha female and supposedly a powerful witch in her own right, but there hadn't been much evidence of her strength to date, and some of the men didn't quite know what to make of her. The rules of dominance were clear, and it was important to shifters to know where everyone stood in the Clan. It made for greater harmony, and dominance battles were often used to settle things.

But nobody was going to challenge Mellie to a fight anytime soon. She had to do something to demonstrate her power or she would continue to make the shifters uncomfortable. They'd do their best to hide it, but it might cause folks to avoid her, which would hurt her feelings. Peter didn't want that. Mellie was dealing with a lot of uncertainty already.

If only her potion would work. Then, her power would be proven, and everyone would know where she fit into the Clan dynamic.

"The magic working done today by Amelia was quite potent," Nansee began her update. "The sentries reported feeling the potion wash over them in a mighty wave of intense magic that felt both benevolent and protective, in the extreme. One said it felt almost exactly like the ward magic, though of a slightly different nature. It seemed to reinforce the ward in some way, sliding along the length of the entire ward wall and creating a larger barrier outward. In other words, it pushed the creatures on the other side of the ward back a great distance, though some of the larger minions and the leviathan itself seemed able to brave the new no-go zone. However, all of the smaller creatures are now much farther away and seem unable to approach, which is a very good result. Sentries will continue to watch and report, but as of the last word, the new barrier is holding strong."

Good news. Peter felt his chest swell with pride on Mellie's behalf. She'd accomplished something with the potion they'd brewed together. He might not be dragon enough to fulfill the letter of the recipe from that old book, but they *had* managed to accomplish something good together. He liked that idea a lot.

Nansee went on a bit longer, but for the most part, the observations had been very positive. The potion had worked to push the smaller creatures away, which was at least more than they had yesterday. Nansee even thanked Mellie for her work and was very gracious about it, which Peter thought was very decent of the mer leader.

Nansee turned the floor back over to John, who looked at Peter with expectation. Summarizing what they had seen, Peter reported what Gus had said and what Peter, himself, had observed and let the council know that Gus continued the watch from on shore. John arranged to have someone relieve Gus and decided they would share out the observation post among several bears for the next day or two until they knew exactly what effects the potion would have long term.

Peter was about to bring up a new topic when Urse burst into the conference room. She was out of breath as if she'd run all the way from the bookshop.

"There's an absolutely giant bear on the beach," Urse said, meeting her mate's gaze. "She's in full view of the street, and I don't recognize her."

"A female?" John asked quickly, his brows drawing together. There weren't a whole lot of female bear shifters in town yet. "Are you sure she's a shifter?"

Urse squinted in thought. "She's so huge, I doubt she

could be anything else."

"What does she look like?" Brody, the sheriff, asked from his seat next to John.

"She's gorgeous. Huge. And her fur is sort of…burgundy-colored," Urse told them.

Peter shot to his feet, and every eye turned to him. "It's all right, my friends. Unless I'm mistaken, my babushka has arrived in town. I'll go tell her the rules, but it's anybody's guess as to whether she'll obey them. My grandmother is a law unto herself."

Peter's smile was wide as he trotted out of the conference room, heading straight for the beach. It wasn't hard to spot the giant bear he hadn't seen is far too long. Peter broke into a jog, then a run.

The bear's head turned and spotted him, and then, she began walking in her stately way, away from the shore and toward her grandson. Time was when his grandmother would have run him down, but she was very old now and moved a little more slowly than she used to.

He was so happy to see her, he ran right up to her, then stopped short.

"Babushka?"

The bear stood on its hind legs and grabbed him in the furriest, most comforting, powerful embrace. Just like he remembered. Peter hugged her back, so happy to have his grandmother near once more.

Mellie squeaked when the massive bear rose on its hind legs and enveloped Peter in enormous paws. Peter was a huge man, but the giant bear made him look small by comparison.

"It's okay. She's just hugging him, not crushing him," John said from Mellie's side.

He'd come outside with the rest of the town council to see what the big Russian female bear looked like. Bears were curious creatures, Mellie had learned. And, when it came to females—even really old ones—they were even more inquisitive.

"She's huge," Mellie whispered, perhaps not all that politely, but she was astounded by the sheer size of the female bear and Peter's ease with her. Mellie could see the affection between them, now that she understood the large bear hadn't been attacking, but welcoming.

"She and Peter are Kamchatka brown bears. The wild ones are nearly as big as Kodiak's, but the coloring is unique. They have that almost violet tint to their fur," John observed. "Of course, Kodiaks are huge in the wild, and the shifter equivalent is even larger. Same goes with Peter's people. But, even among their Clan, his babushka and all her descendants are something special."

"Have you met Peter's family before?" Urse asked her husband.

"A few of them, but never his granny. He's told us all stories about her for years, of course. She's quite a character and very protective of her territory and kin." John looked on in approval as the bear and man broke apart and started walking together down the beach toward the far end of the cove where Peter's den was located. Everybody turned back toward the town hall, now that the show was over, and Mellie followed along with her sister and John.

"Peter told us about how, a decade or so ago, some humans wanted to set up a platinum mine on the edge of her territory. Not sure what they did, but it was something really bad, and two of the human guards ended up dead. Then, the Clan—about thirty bears strong—besieged the compound and wouldn't let the humans out for weeks." Brody chuckled, as did the others within hearing.

"That mining company lost a lot of money when the workers couldn't leave their homes to work for weeks on end," John elaborated. "Finally, they relented and stuck to their original agreement with Peter's grandmother. She'd signed a contract with them in human form as the land owner, but the mine bosses had taken shortcuts that were detrimental to the land. When Granny had no luck making the miners stick to the contract terms, she went bear on their asses until they gave in. Very effective negotiating strategy."

"It's funny in light of the fact that the Kamchatkas are usually seen as teddy bears. They rarely attack humans—probably because most of those that interact with humans are shifters. The true bears are more elusive because of hunting. They've learned to evade humans," Brody said conversationally. "The shifters could evade the hunters, too, of course, but they run interference, trying to protect the wild bears."

Mellie felt for the helpless bears, even if they weren't shifters. It sounded like they just wanted to live their lives in peace and weren't a threat to humans, so the idea that humans hunted the bears for sport really irked her. Some people were just cruel.

Mellie went home with Urse and John after the meeting broke up, joining her sister and the Alpha bear for dinner. The afternoon had slipped away from them, and the bookstore had been closed since Urse came running to town hall. It could stay closed for the rest of the day. It wasn't like Grizzly Cove was bustling with tourists yet. They would come…eventually. When the town—and the bear shifter population—was ready for them.

*

The next morning, Peter was feeling eager. He wasn't sure how the day was going to go, but he had a plan, and he was going to put it into motion. Babushka had settled into the guest room in his den he had prepared with her in mind, and they had spent the evening catching up on news from the family and the Clan back in the old country.

She'd also told him all about her trip here. She'd come to the States in the company of three of his cousins. They had wanted to see her all the way to Grizzly Cove, but she had demurred. She hadn't wanted to descend on the American bears *en masse*. It wasn't polite, she'd insisted, so she'd had them drop her off in Seattle, and she'd made her way here by herself. That included renting a four-wheel drive vehicle, that she'd parked on Main Street when she'd felt the need to go furry.

Peter had retrieved the rental car and parked it in his drive. He'd also retrieved all her luggage and carried it into his den. He couldn't explain the feeling of home his grandmother had brought with her, but with her in his house, it truly felt like a home for the first time. Only one thing was missing…and he hoped to settle that to some extent tonight.

He left his grandmother at the den. She was sleeping late after her travels and had all she needed in the house for when she rose. Bears were independent by nature, and he knew she wouldn't appreciate him hovering over her. Giving her some space and time on her own was probably the best thing he could do at this point.

That in mind, Peter headed for Main Street, stopping off at the bakery to get some treats on his way to the bookstore. He had to open the butcher shop later. He'd been letting the guys in town take stuff on the honor system for the past few days—as he often did—but every once in a while, he had to do paperwork and place orders from some of his suppliers.

First, though, he had to complete his self-appointed mission. He headed for the bookshop, bakery box in hand. When he walked in the door, the little bell above it tinkled his arrival, and Mellie looked up from her seated position at the desk in the back of the shop. She'd been working on the computer, and the soft glow of the screen lit her face in an ethereal light. The smile she sent him warmed him from the inside out.

"Good morning," she said, rising from her seat and moving toward him.

"These are for you," Peter said somewhat awkwardly, raising the box in his hand to bring her attention to it.

Mellie's eyes widened. "What did you do? Clean out the bakery?"

He looked at the large box and wondered if he'd overestimated on the number of pastries to order. "Is it too much? This is the size I usually get."

Mellie chuckled. "Bear size," she told him, but didn't seem upset by his mistake. "There's plenty to share, if you can spare a few minutes. Or have you eaten already?"

No way was he going to admit to having eaten anything this morning, even if he'd been up since dawn. "I would be happy to join you," he said, following her toward the countertop where she usually rang up purchases.

Mellie took charge, placing the box on the counter and using scissors she had near the cash register to clip the strings holding the box closed. She opened it and carefully unlatched the side flaps to make it sit flat on the countertop. The aromas of sugar, honey and various sorts of toppings and fillings came to him at once, making his nose twitch. The trio of sisters who ran the bakery really did know how to cook. Peter's mouth watered, even as Mellie pulled out paper plates and napkins from behind the counter.

"Grab that stool," she told Peter, pointing toward a cushioned stool off to one side as Mellie grabbed a matching one from behind the counter. "Urse and I do this all the time since we don't have a lot of foot traffic in the store yet," she told him. "Rather than close up the shop when we want to nosh, we just decided to put a stash of the necessary utensils and accoutrements under here." She gave him a conspiratorial smile as she handed him a paper plate and napkin.

"Very efficient," he complimented her. "But, if John's plans for the town come to fruition, there will be more foot traffic come tourist season."

"Yeah, I know. I'm not entirely sure whether or not to be happy about that. I've sort of grown used to the town the way it is, and I like the slower pace," she admitted.

"But you'll make more money if you have more customers, no?"

"Sure, but there's more to life than making money," she replied, touching a chord in his own heart, though she probably didn't realize it. "You guys have got a pretty sweet thing going here. A town where shifters can be shifters and your grandmother can waltz down the beach in bear form without ten guys with tranquilizer rifles being called out to shoot her."

Peter barked a laugh at the image she painted with her words. "You're right," he told her, between chuckles. "We all know that it can't go on forever, though. Eventually, humans will start showing up in greater numbers. At the moment, we only get the occasional tourist, but word is already spreading about our sweet little artists' colony here. Brody's chainsaw masterpieces aside, Lyn Ling's bamboo art gallery has drawn attention from Northern Californian art critics, and she's even got a brisk mail order business beginning to take off. I helped her a bit with the website."

"I've seen it," Mellie told him excitedly. "Love the graphics."

"That's all Lyn. I just helped with the menu scripts and the shopping cart," he replied modestly. He'd done quite a bit more than that, but he wasn't a braggart.

"Well, maybe when we have time to breathe again, you can help out a bit with the bookstore's site," she said with a trace of humor. "We had this idea of featuring postcards, notecards, stationary—heck, even T-shirts—with some of the best art from cove residents and selling it online and in the store to supplement our book income."

"Sounds like a good idea," Peter told her, glad to hear the sisters were putting thought into their business in addition to their magical work for the town. "I bet John will like this plan."

"He does. Urse talked it over with him already, though it's only in the planning stages. He thought it might attract more tourists, which is the eventual plan, of course. But the timing… Urse may have completed her task, but there's still a lot to do on my part. And the town itself isn't quite ready yet for throngs of the general public. With any luck, we'll be ready about the same time the town is, so it's an idea we're deferring for a few months, at least."

"I will help with the website whenever you want to start

setting it up," he told her, glad to be able to help her in any way she needed.

"Thanks, that's really nice of you." The smile she favored him with warmed his heart. "Now, which of these do you want?" She pointed to the selection of a dozen different pastries.

"You go first," he said graciously. "I like them all."

"Well, in that case…" Mellie made a small production out of choosing just the right pastry, lifting it in her fingers and taking it directly to her mouth for as big a bite as she could manage. Peter watched her every move, wishing that little pink tongue would lick out at him sometime, just the way she licked the stray icing off her own plump lips.

Could a guy get a boner just from watching a woman eat a honey bun? Apparently, he could. Peter shifted his position on the stool, hoping to ease the sudden tightness of his jeans. Mellie didn't appear to notice his discomfort. She was too busy making love to the pastry he'd brought for her.

Sweet Goddess in heaven! He might come just from watching her eat, which was an entirely new experience for him. Never before had he known a woman to be so innocently sensual. Her every move made his lust rise higher.

Whoa, boy. He had to get better control over his responses, or this hunt might be over before it even truly began.

Realizing he'd been staring, Peter picked a pastry at random and crammed half of it in his face so she wouldn't catch him staring at her like some sort of pervert. Raspberry. Not his absolute favorite, but not bad. Peter chewed, enjoying the burst of flavor, which only seemed to heighten his arousal. Damn.

"How is your grandmother settling in?" Mellie asked between bites. "I bet she's happy to see you again."

"She is. But she likes her space, too. She is reserving judgment about this town, but she's very intrigued about how it all works. Where we come from, we have a more dense arrangement of bears than is usual in the rest of the world. Our Clan is pretty tight, and we like living closer to each other than most other bear shifters. But this… So many different bears in such close proximity. Babushka is skeptical, but she said the idea appeals to her in these times of trouble. There is safety in numbers, she says."

"A wise woman," Mellie agreed. "So, that's why you're here? You're giving Grandma some space?"

"Yes," he affirmed. "That, and I really have to open the shop today and catch up on paperwork. Plus, I wanted to invite you to dinner at my home tonight." Here it was. The real reason he'd come to the bookstore and gathered his courage. "Grandmother might be able to help you with your quest," he offered, hoping to sweeten the invitation. "She knew the dragon in our family line when she was a young girl. She might be able to tell you a bit more about him or, at least, about dragons in general." He shrugged. The idea was thin, but it was the best he could come up with to try to convince her to eat dinner with him and his grandmother.

The real reasons behind his invitation would probably scare her off. He wanted the first contact between his babushka and his potential mate to be in private. That way, if there was a problem, he could try to contain it and not let the entire cove know that his grandmother had a problem with *strega*.

"Oh, that sounds great," Mellie enthused. "I'd love to join you for dinner. Can I bring anything?"

"Just your beautiful self," he told her in a moment of unguarded candor. He held his breath. She didn't seem to mind his compliment. In fact, she seemed to glow at his words, her smile turning a shade self-conscious, perhaps, but overall, she looked very pleased.

He ate another three pastries before one of the loner bear shifters who lived way back in the woods entered the store. Mellie saw that she had a customer and jumped guiltily from her seat.

"Mr. Bender! I have your special order in back. Let me just go get your books." Mellie rushed into the backroom, and Peter stood uncomfortably, putting his stool back where he'd found it. He nodded to the newcomer.

"Samuel."

"Peter." The newcomer acknowledged the greeting with a nod of his head then looked around the bookshop in an unconvincing show of nonchalance. "So… You and Mel?"

Peter's eyes narrowed. Was Samuel interested in Mellie? If that was the case, Peter would make the other man bleed.

"What if it is?" Peter challenged, but Samuel held up his hands, palms outward.

"No skin off my nose," he said quickly. "I like the sisters, but I doubt I'll ever find a mate. I'm too ornery for my own good." Samuel smiled crookedly, and Peter relaxed marginally. "Mel gets me the books I want and never asks too many probing questions about why a bear shifter is so interested in theoretical physics, or what have you."

"Well, do me a favor and keep it to yourself for now," Peter requested in a friendlier tone. "I'm not entirely sure this is going to work out."

"I heard your granny caused a stir when she arrived yesterday," Samuel observed, his eyes gleaming with humor. "Is she why you're not so sure about you and Mel?"

"Could be. Could be I'm not sure Mellie will have me with all my faults. I'm not really sure if humans—even mages—can feel the same way we do," Peter revealed, saying more to Samuel than he'd expected to reveal.

"Try not to overthink it too much," Samuel advised. "I have no doubt the older sister is devoted to Big John."

Peter had to admit Samuel had a good point. He would have said so, but at that moment, Mellie returned carrying a large stack of books. Peter didn't even try to read the titles. He was sure the esoteric nature of Samuel's reading choices would be noteworthy, but Peter was more interested in the woman holding the books than in the books themselves.

Peter had hoped to leave Mellie with a kiss to remember him by, but Samuel's presence had ruined his plans. It didn't look like the man was going to leave anytime soon, either. He had produced a handwritten list of books he wanted Mellie to order for him, and she was asking him to clarify the chicken scratch Samuel called handwriting. That could take a while.

"I'll see you later," Peter interjected during a brief pause in the conversation while Mellie was looking up a title on her computer.

Mellie looked up and smiled at him. "What should I wear?"

"Come as you are," he told her. "In fact, I'll swing by after work and pick you up."

"Sounds good," she told him. "See you then."

Peter strutted out the door, feeling ten feet tall. She hadn't minded Samuel knowing that they were seeing each other later. That was a good sign. At least, he took it as one.

CHAPTER SIX

Mellie was walking on air the rest of the day. She had a date with Peter! Sure, his grandmother would be there as a very effective chaperone, but maybe, in a way, that might be better. Otherwise, she was liable to dive in head first and sleep with the man. Not that it wasn't a good idea and something she'd been thinking about for months now, but she was still hesitant.

What if she tried to jump his bones, and he wasn't really that interested? What if they did the deed, and then, he walked away, unmoved…uninvolved? What if she lost her heart to the man, and he didn't want it? Mellie was very much afraid she'd already lost little pieces of her heart to him, and she just hoped he wouldn't throw them away.

She tried on a few different outfits before going back to what she'd been wearing in the shop earlier, just a little jazzed up with a pretty scarf and some jewelry. She didn't want to look as if she'd made a fuss, but she also wanted to make a good impression on Peter's grandmother.

What did it mean that he was inviting her over to meet his grandmother? That thought hit her like lightning about midway through her indecisive primping. Had he invited her simply to meet his grandma so the older woman could tell Mellie what she knew about dragons? Or had there been more to his invitation? Had he specifically wanted her to meet his grandmother for some reason? The thought made her giddy.

Meeting a guy's family was a serious step. Was that the step they were taking, or was it just circumstance making this happen and she was reading way too much into it? Mellie tried to scold herself that she had to be a grownup about this, but the giggly teenager that still lived inside her thought otherwise.

Pulling a bottle of red wine out of the rack, Mellie put it into one of the gift bags they sold in the bookshop. The least she could do was bring it along, even though Peter had told her she didn't have to bring anything. It was a small enough token, and she was pretty sure whatever Peter served for dinner would include red meat of some kind, so red wine was a pretty sure bet.

When Peter walked into the shop at about closing time, Urse had—thankfully—already left. Her older sister was working abbreviated hours lately, but Mellie didn't mind. Urse had taken a lot of time to recover from casting those permanent wards, and since then, she'd been enjoying a bit of a honeymoon with her mate. Mellie didn't begrudge her sister that time with John. Not when John made her sister happier than Mellie had ever seen her.

At least one of them was getting laid on a regular basis. More than regular, if the sappy smile on Urse's face meant anything. Just that morning, Urse had been a couple of hours late, and Mellie just knew why. Urse had that satisfied glow about her, and she'd smiled all morning at nothing. Yeah, that was the look of a satisfied woman, and Urse had been wearing that expression for a while now. Mellie was amused by it, even as she was a little bit jealous.

Mellie greeted Peter from behind the counter and called out that she was just going to lock up the back. She grabbed the bag with the bottle of wine from where she'd left it in the backroom and grabbed her coat. Turning back, she was surprised to find Peter had joined her, and he had a hungry look on his face. A hungry look that set her insides on fire.

"I'm sorry I left without doing this before," he told her even as he swept his arms around her waist and tugged her close. Then, he bent her backward as his lips descended, taking hers in a devastatingly romantic gesture that made her want to swoon right there on the spot.

The kiss wasn't bad either. Peter rocked her world off its axis and sent her senses to orbit before she even had a chance to catch her breath. When he finally let her up…slowly…she was dazed. Completely befuddled by the instantaneous passion only he had ever inspired in her.

"Wow," she breathed, smiling when he did.

"Wow, indeed," he agreed, standing her up and holding her until she was steadier on her feet. "Are you ready to go?" he asked in low tone that was more heavily accented than usual. "If we stay here much longer, we might not make it to my place, and Babushka is waiting for us."

Brought back to her senses by the reminder of her duty, Mellie stepped away from him. "I'm ready," she told him, trying to rein in her wayward libido.

This simply wasn't the time or place for what she craved. She had to be patient…and cautious. She still wasn't sure what endgame he had in mind, and much as she wanted to be with him, she was very much afraid that, after being with Peter, she would never be the same.

They walked in companionable silence out to the street where Peter had parked his truck. He drove a big pickup that was more comfortable than Mellie had expected.

"I've never ridden in a pickup truck before," she said as he helped her into the passenger seat.

"Seriously?" Peter looked surprised.

"Not many of them in San Francisco, I guess. At least not among my circle of friends." She shrugged, already looking around the cab of the truck.

There were so many knobs and buttons, not to mention what looked like a touchscreen, the cab looked more like a pilot's cockpit than the cab of a simple pickup truck. Peter made sure she was in and her door closed before he made his way around to the driver's side.

"What is all this?" Mellie asked, gesturing toward the complicated dashboard.

Peter looked a little sheepish. "I may have modified things a bit."

"Please tell me you didn't put in an ejection seat," she joked, and he laughed with her.

"No. No ejection seat, though it was tempting," he admitted.

He started the truck and drove toward his home. Mellie wasn't too steady after that soul-shattering kiss, so small talk was hard. It didn't matter, though. Peter was good company whether they were talking or not. He drove for a while in silence, seeming comfortable with it. It was only when they neared his property that he started telling her about some of the modifications he'd made to his vehicle.

"The truck came with three little buttons for garage door openers, but I needed more. Basically, they're just little transmitters, and I have a lot of security equipment that can respond to such signals. For example, if I touch this button…" He reached over and pushed a small black button on the modified dash. "That disarms the motion sensors on the driveway as we approach." He pushed a few more buttons but didn't explain each and every function. If these buttons controlled aspects of his home alarm systems, she didn't blame him for not sharing too much information.

Not that she could have used any of it anyway. None of the buttons were labelled. Only Peter would know which buttons to push and when. All in all, she was impressed with his ingenuity.

"I hope you like steak," Peter said as he pulled up in the drive before a lovely log cabin that seemed to fit right into its surroundings. There was a calmness about the place. A gentleness that spoke to Mellie.

"Love it. And, Peter…" She looked all around, but especially at the house. "I love what you've done here. There's something very special about this place." Her magical senses reached out, and what she found was unexpected. "It's as if the trees themselves welcome you," she said, a bit of awe in her tone that she couldn't hide.

"Truly?" he asked, getting out of the truck then coming around to her side to help her down. "That's what I was going for, but I couldn't be a hundred percent sure, though I believe the redwoods have come to accept me."

"You're aware of the consciousness of trees?" she asked in a low voice, surprised in the extreme.

"It makes sense. It always has, to me at least." He shrugged as she slid down to the ground from the high seat, then closed the door behind her.

"Very few people in my experience give credence to the living nature of all creation," she told him.

"It's all the same to me. I built this cabin out of deadfall. I didn't kill any trees to make my home, and I don't cut down trees for firewood. It just didn't seem right," he admitted.

"You must be especially sensitive to have felt that," she said, looking again at the bear-man who was fast capturing every last corner of her heart.

Peter shrugged again. "I follow my instincts."

He had parked so that the passenger door faced the front door of the cabin. Peter kept hold of her hand as they walked toward the front door.

When the door opened to reveal an older woman who was taller than Mellie and was unmistakably Peter's relative, Mellie almost stopped short in surprise. She would have, if Peter hadn't been holding her hand and kept moving forward. She had to keep up with him or tug her hand free—which was out of the question for many reasons, but mostly because she liked holding hands with him a little too much to let go easily.

"Peter," the older woman said, speaking to him but looking with curious eyes at Mellie the whole time. "Who have you brought to meet me?"

"Babushka, this is Amelia Ricoletti. She is a witch. A *strega*."

"*Italiano*?" the older woman asked Mellie.

"Italian-American," Mellie replied with a self-conscious smile. "My nonna settled in San Francisco before my mother was born. She adopted this country as her own but never let go the ways of the old country. My sister and I were raised as *strega* from the moment it became known we shared her gift."

"Sister?" Now, Peter's grandmother looked to her grandson for clarification.

"John's new mate, Ursula. She who cast the permanent wards to keep the town and cove safe," Peter told her, as if he was repeating something he'd already told her.

"Ah, yes," his grandmother said, turning back to Mellie with a welcoming smile. "I remember now. I am Ivana. Let's see… You already have a nonna. You can call me granny."

"Babushka!" Peter seemed shocked, but the older woman just waved him off.

"What?" Ivana looked askance at her grandson. "I don't think she speaks Russian, does she? And I have always fancied the thought of being an American granny. Perhaps I will ask the whole town to call me that. I suspect I am the oldest bear here."

Granny Ivana chuckled at her own idea, and Mellie found the sound contagious. "Honestly, sometimes, I think the boys could use a little adult supervision," Mellie said to the older woman in a conspiratorial tone, which only made her laugh harder.

Mellie felt an instant kinship with the woman who had asked her to call her granny. This was a woman of quick humor who seemed to be welcoming. Mellie had been so scared to meet Peter's grandmother, but Granny Ivana set her immediately at ease.

"Come, come," Granny Ivana said, stepping aside to usher them through the doorway and into Peter's home as if it was her own.

As Mellie entered, Granny Ivana enveloped her in a welcoming hug and kissed both cheeks. She was a lot taller than Mellie and more substantial. Her bear hug in human form brought a feeling of care and comfort Mellie had only ever felt before from her own nonna.

Mellie's instincts about people were often spot on, and they were telling her that Granny Ivana was a very special, very caring lady. Mellie liked the older woman and hoped the feeling was mutual. With a granny like this, she wasn't surprised Peter had grown up to be the sensitive fellow he was—who had gone so far as to harm no trees in the building of his home.

That alone told her there was much more to Peter than met the eye. The other bear shifters might be sensitive to magic and hold more magic of their own than almost any other kind of shifter, but Peter was something special. That he could feel the spirits of the trees—something on such a different wavelength than most people and animals… Well, maybe it was the dragon-blood influence showing up, after all.

And thinking of dragons made her think of her task. Maybe Granny Ivana could help. Now, having met the woman, Mellie was pretty much convinced that, if she knew anything, Granny Ivana would at least try to help.

Peter went right to work, setting up to grill a number of different exotic meats from his shop while Mellie offered to help Granny Ivana with the salad and side dishes. Granny set her right to work, setting the table while they talked of life in the cove and Granny's trip to the States.

It had, apparently, been quite an adventure, in the company of three of Peter's cousins. Granny had left the cousins behind at some point and come the rest of the way on her own over the younger generation's objections.

"I suspect they tried to follow me for a time," Granny Ivana admitted with a twinkle in her eye. "But I was learning stealth and diversion long before Peter and his cousins were born. I wonder which one of them was able to track me longest?"

"I bet on Xander. He has skills," Peter put in from his place at the fancy indoor grill.

"Really? I was thinking Yuri, but I suppose I could be wrong," Granny Ivana said in a contemplative tone. "The last I saw any of them, they'd all bought big motorcycles and had planned to hit the open road, as they called it. I encouraged them to explore. I'm hoping they'll find mates and settle down. Lady knows, they've been through almost every girl in Russia, Europe and the Middle East," Granny Ivana griped with a laugh.

"You think they'll find mates here?" Peter asked, clearly curious.

Granny shrugged. "If Nikita is right, they all will," she replied to Peter, then looked at Mellie. "Nikita is a family friend. She is like you. *Ved'ma.* A witch. We were girls together in Kamchatka."

Mellie was relieved to hear directly from Peter's grandmother that she didn't have a problem with witches. Regardless of what he'd said about his granny and the witchy *ved'ma* she'd consulted from time to time in the old country, Mellie had been wary. Magic users weren't always welcome—in fact, they usually weren't welcome—among shifters. Grizzly Cove was a little different, thankfully. Though the town council hadn't expected the Ricoletti sisters to be witches when they'd approved the plans for the bookstore, Urse had managed to smooth things over. The fact that she was the Alpha bear's true mate went a long way toward gaining acceptance for both Urse and Mellie in the town.

There was some bustling as Peter finished with the grill and served up a heaping platter of seared meats. Mellie's little steak was cooked well-done, but the others were another matter. Seemed both Peter and his granny liked their meats on the rare side. Mellie supposed that was the bear influence, and she tried not to stare as he loaded giant plates for both himself and his granny with three or four cuts of various kinds of meat, each.

Mellie's single steak looked paltry by comparison, though she loaded the empty part of her plate with broiled potatoes and salad. They all ate for a while, Peter pointing out various varieties of meat he'd served his grandmother. They discussed the finer points of taste and texture like connoisseurs while Mellie worked on her own meal. She shouldn't have been surprised at how much the bear shifters could eat. She'd seen her new brother-in-law pack it away many times now. But, somehow, she'd expected Granny Ivana to eat less. Instead, she ate more than Peter!

Then again, her bear was massive, and the woman herself wasn't petite in her human form. She wasn't quite six feet tall, but she was definitely way taller than Mellie, and bigger boned, as well, though Granny Ivana was in no way fat or even overweight. Shifters generally weren't, to Mellie's knowledge. All that activity while they were in their animal forms, and the huge amount of energy it must take just to shift in the first place, kept them lean and muscular. Lucky shifters.

"So," Granny Ivana said after she'd finished most of her meal. She sat back and looked at Mellie with piercing dark eyes as she lingered over the last bits on her plate. "Peter tells me you are in need of a dragon."

Mellie almost choked at the older woman's directness but managed to keep a straight face. "I am. Though, I didn't even realize dragon shifters existed—or once existed—before talking with Peter."

Granny Ivana nodded sagely. "He told me of your experiment with his blood." She smiled with satisfaction. "While I am pleased with the results of the potion you two brewed together, it seems clear you all need something…different than bear blood in your next attempt. While I would be willing to give you my own blood, I believe it was Peter's personal investment in the fate of this place that allowed for the success of your previous attempt. My grandfather was a dragon, but I am fully bear, as you may have seen."

Mellie's spirits rose and fell with Granny Ivana's words. What was she saying? Would she help or wouldn't she?

"While I may not be the best to help directly, I may be able to help you locate a dragon shifter," Granny Ivana went on.

Mellie sat straight up in her chair. "There's a dragon? Alive? Now?"

"There might be," Granny Ivana said with a slight frown. "At least, I knew of one once, but we'll have to track him down. If he still exists."

"Shifter grapevine?" Peter asked at once, but Granny Ivana shook her head.

"If he lives, other shifters will not know of his animal. Dragons were hunted by everyone—other shifters included. They are too powerful, and many fear them," Granny told him. "No, for this, we need to consult the magical grapevine, so to speak. We'll start with Nikita and see where she sends us. I hope you get a good rate for long-distance calls," she added with a wink.

CHAPTER SEVEN

A few minutes later, Granny Ivana was speaking in rapid-fire Russian with her friend, Nikita, back in Kamchatka. Peter was listening intently, so Mellie didn't bother him to ask for a translation. She just tried to sit quietly and be as patient as possible while, inside, she was in a turmoil of curiosity.

To give herself something to do, Mellie went back to the table that they'd recently vacated in favor of the living room area and its phone, and started to clean up the dinner dishes. She stacked them as quietly as possible and brought them to the sink, going about the routine chores in an effort to calm her nerves. When she heard the phone receiver click down into the cradle, she spun around, unable to contain her excitement, but Granny Ivana's expression gave no clues about the outcome of her phone call.

"Well?" Mellie demanded of Peter. He glanced back to his grandmother.

"Nikita's last knowledge of his whereabouts ends in Italy," Granny Ivana revealed.

"Italy!" Mellie's mind raced with ideas. "We can call Nonna. She has really good contacts there."

Granny Ivana offered the phone to Mellie, but she demurred, pulling her cell from her pocketbook instead. "I have Nonna's number programmed in here, and she'll know it's me calling from this number," Mellie explained, even as she connected the call.

Nonna didn't seem surprised by Mellie's call, though Mellie felt some satisfaction at being able to ask for something Nonna hadn't anticipated. Good granny that she was, though, she readily agreed to call her friends in Italy as soon as possible. Mellie then handed the phone to Granny Ivana so she could pass on the details firsthand.

Mellie and Peter shared a wide-eyed look when the two grandmothers were speaking. It sure sounded as if they were old friends, and when the conversation went from English to Italian, Mellie was astonished to learn that Granny Ivana had spent time in Turin and Parma during her long life and still spoke the language very well indeed.

Granny Ivana ended the call and handed the silent phone back to Mellie with a broad smile. "Very sensible woman, your nonna," Granny complimented. "I should like to meet her in person one day."

"We've been asking her to come up for a visit to see the shop and the town, but she claims the time isn't right yet," Mellie said. "Urse thinks I have to do my part to protect the place first, and only then, will Nonna come. Nothing like a little more pressure, right?" Mellie gave a nervous laugh as she put her phone away.

"Try not to stress about it, *vnuchka*. What will be, will be. Worrying about it cannot help," Granny Ivana said. Mellie knew just enough Russian to be charmed that Granny Ivana had called her granddaughter. "Now, let me tell you a few things about dragons, should your nonna succeed. You will have to approach cautiously. Dragons are not like us cuddly bears. They are secretive and deadly."

Mellie sobered immediately. This woman had actually known a dragon shifter. She, and her grandson, were related to a dragon shifter. They were as close as Mellie had ever come to a dragon, and she would take any advice she could get.

They sat in the living room, sipping coffee and watching while Peter stoked the fire in the fireplace. Granny Ivana held court.

"My grandfather was a dragon. Bartolomeo was his name. He was Italian, which was why I traveled to that country in my youth, to try to track down his people, but I had no success."

"Wait a minute. My great-grandfather was Italian?" Peter asked, coming over to sit next to Mellie on the couch.

"You didn't know?" Mellie blurted out, unable to help herself.

In her family, lineage was everything. Even though the *strega* gift was passed down through the female line, she knew as much about her paternal ancestors as she could. It seemed impossible to her that Peter wouldn't know such a crucial fact as the origins of his ancestors.

"It's not his fault." Granny Ivana was quick to come to her grandson's defense. "We don't talk much about the dragon. Only that he existed, and only in strict confidence. Dragons were hunted long before the Destroyer made killing them into a sport. Bartolomeo was one of very few dragons in the world during his time, and for the most part, he hid his nature from everyone but those closest to him. When he came to Kamchatka, he found his mate in my grandmother, Nadia, but he also found acceptance among our people in a place that few humans ever visited. Kamchatka, even to this day, is sparsely populated, and way back when Bartolomeo and Nadia lived there, it was even quieter. He could fly when he wished and not worry about being hunted. The entire Clan was on his side, protecting him and his secret. The secret of our family. It is not something we speak of often, even among ourselves."

Mellie realized the gift Granny Ivana was giving her in telling her all this. "I will never speak of your ancestors or your family to anyone but Peter or yourself, Granny. This I swear." Mellie put a little charge of magic into her oath that Granny Ivana and Peter could probably scent, being highly magical bears themselves.

Granny Ivana nodded with satisfaction. "I believe you, which is why I speak of these things. Also, I think you need to know this in order to complete your task and help make my grandson, his chosen comrades, and all those that come under their protection safe from the evil in the sea."

Mellie nodded respectfully. Granny Ivana truly did understand all that was at stake here and was being incredibly gracious. She went on at length, describing the quirks of her grandfather and the things that would upset him. She also talked about his need to fly and how he did so without attracting unwanted attention.

"Dragons are more mobile than almost any other shifter," Granny Ivana told her. "They can cover more ground in less time than any bird shifter and fly higher than any other creature. Bartolomeo was born in Italy but had travelled the world before finding Nadia. That she was of Kamchatka worked out well for him because of the isolation and the protective nature of our Clan. They welcomed him into the Clan and protected his secret."

Mellie was hanging on every word. This was a woman who had actually known a real live dragon shifter. She had experience and knowledge that could be invaluable to Mellie in her quest to find that final ingredient.

It wasn't just an ingredient she was after. It wasn't like finding an herb in the forest and picking it at exactly the right moment. No, this substance had to be obtained directly from a living, thinking, feeling, possibly elusive creature. A person with ideas and demands of their own. Mellie would have to deal with that person in both human and dragon form, if she was to complete her task.

Knowing as much as she could about dragon shifters and their quirks as possible might prove vital. Granny Ivana's willingness to help prepare her for a possible encounter with a dragon shifter—and especially her helpfulness in trying to track one down—was an amazing gift. Mellie had already decided to like Peter's grandmother, but now, she was coming to respect and admire her, as well.

"Dragons have never had an easy time of it in the mortal world," Granny Ivana went on. "They're so big and scary." She laughed at her own description. "Of course, people say that about us, too, but we're not so visible, stalking in the woods, as they are flying high above in the sky. They're very vulnerable until they achieve a certain height, or can find cloud cover to hide behind. On land, they are immense in comparison to most creatures. Very hard to hide, which is why, I think, they enjoy cave systems so much."

"Have they always been hunted?" Peter asked.

"As far back as I know, yes," Granny Ivana confirmed. "Although, there are legends, even among humans, about the time when they were friends and comrades with kings and mages alike. The legend of Merlin and Arthur comes to mind, and there are other stories from the east of dragons transporting emperors in China and elsewhere. Dragon sages and mages."

Mellie's imagination had been captured by the tales of Camelot, Arthur and Merlin when she was a young girl. The idea that the dragons in the old stories might actually have been real was like something out of a fairytale. Magical and unexpected. She felt almost giddy at the prospect of meeting such a mysterious being. Excited and, at the same time, scared to death. Dragons devoured young maidens, didn't they?

"I don't know what kind of dragon we may find in this day and age. They have not had it easy for the past few centuries. It would be wise to approach with caution and utmost respect for the fact that he is more deadly than any other shifter in existence. Peter," Granny Ivana spoke to her grandson, "you must go with her if she finds the dragon. You must protect her. We Kamchatka have great magic of our own, and you have dragon blood. You might be the only thing that can stand between her and an enraged dragon for any length of time."

Peter nodded, his face deathly serious. "I will not let her out of my sight should we encounter a dragon."

"Good." Granny Ivana rose, signaling the end of their conversation. "Now, take the girl home and see that she is safe before you return. I will not wait up." Granny sent Mellie a teasing wink and walked out of the living room toward the back of the house where Mellie guessed the bedrooms were located.

Just like that, she and Peter were alone. She looked at him, eyebrows raised in question. "I guess that's that, then." She chuckled as he did.

"Babushka is used to being the Alpha female in all things. She can be abrupt, but as you see, every action is made with love," Peter told her as they rose and headed toward the coat rack by the door. "I suspect she left us alone so that we might talk without her influence. She knows how big her presence is and how she becomes the center of attention wherever she is. It is a power she wields wisely and with compassion."

Peter helped Mellie into her coat and then ushered her out the door and back into his truck. They drove away from the house, making small talk.

"I really enjoyed dinner, and your grandmother is incredible," Mellie said, watching the trees go by in the dark night. Peter's house was way out toward one tip of the cove, near the standing stones she'd been to the day before while casting that potion they'd made together.

"I think she hit it off with your nonna," he replied, sending her a smile across the width of the truck cab.

"Goddess help us all if those two ever get together," Mellie said, laughing. "Nonna is like a toned-down version of your granny. Quieter on the outside, but there's a raging torrent of power just under the surface. She can be scary, though, as you described with Granny Ivana, everything Nonna does comes from a place of love. Even when she's teaching you a lesson."

"I can only imagine how magical folk discipline their

kids," Peter mused. "Did she turn you into a newt?"

Mellie laughed aloud. "No, though there was the odd threat of transmutation when we were too little to understand how difficult such spells really were to cast. Mostly, she would lock down certain aspects of our power until we learned the right way to use it. Every magical child is unique with a unique set of gifts. As they develop, depending on the child's age, they may or may not understand the right or wrong way to use a certain ability. It's the parent or guardian's role to make sure the child learns restraint and the ethical use of certain skills before they're allowed to run wild with them. Like…say Urse or I were mindreaders…"

"You're not, are you?" Peter asked quickly.

"No. Neither of us have that gift. But say one of us did and it manifested when we were too young to understand the ethics of traipsing through someone else's thoughts. If that happened, and Nonna found out we were using our new powers without thought for consequences, or to harm another being, she would punish us by cutting off that power until it was just a harmless trickle. She would then set about showing us, in no uncertain terms, why that power should be used only under the correct conditions and with the utmost care. Being cut off from your natural power is a punishment for magical children. You feel incomplete and sort of…bereft…while your magic is locked down. Believe me, you learn fast how to do the right thing."

Peter pulled up in back of the bookstore, by the entrance that led to the apartment above. Unlike some of the other shops in town, the bookstore had been built so that the only way to access the staircase that led up to the apartment was through the backroom of the shop. Some of the other buildings had separate outdoor entrances to the upper level, but the shops designed for human ownership were a bit more secure to protect both the humans and the shifters. Of course, when Mellie and her sister had signed on to open the bookshop, nobody had realized they were witches. That revelation had come later and had posed a bit of an issue for a short time before the girls showed how devoted they were to the safety of the town, cove and all the beings who lived there.

Peter helped Mellie down from the truck and walked her to the back door of the shop. She used her key to open the door to the back storeroom of the building, and Peter went in to make sure it was as she had left it hours before. Mellie came in behind him, shut the outer door, and together, they walked toward the staircase.

"Do you want to come up? I have cappuccino, wine, or the beer I keep on hand for John, when he comes over for dinner with Urse." Mellie was a little nervous.

She knew, if she got him up to her apartment, things might progress into more...adventurous...places from there. She hoped they would. But did he want to? And, if he wanted to, was he thinking fling or long-term?

There was no way to know, and she almost wished she had a bit of that mindreading talent she'd mentioned before. It would make this all so much easier if she knew what his intentions were toward her. Did they have a chance at something lasting or was this strictly an as-you-go sort of encounter?

Frankly, at this point, she didn't really care either way. At least, not right at that moment. No, right now, her senses were crying out for his touch, his kiss...and a whole lot more.

"I'd like that," he told her, his words casual, but his gaze intense. Something deep down jumped for joy that he'd accepted her invitation.

She preceded him up the stairs and felt his gaze on her the entire length of the flight of stairs. Mellie unlocked the door at the top—there were deadbolts on the doors at both ends of the staircase—and walked into the dark apartment. Before she could even hit the switch for the light, Peter's arms came around her from behind, hauling her close against his chest. His lips were at her ear when he spoke in a low, urgent whisper.

"Do you want me as much as I want you?" he asked, her

stomach flipping at the sudden urgency. Her answer, of course, was an emphatic *yes*, but she tried to play it cooler than that.

She turned in his arms and showed him rather than told him, raising her hands to either side of his face and lifting her lips to his. She was aware of motion as she lost herself in his kiss but only realized he'd turned her around when her back came up against the closed door. Peter had kicked it shut and then spun them so he could press her against the solid wood in one of the sexiest moves she had ever been part of. If he wasn't holding her up, she might've swooned right then and there.

He took his time, seducing her with his mouth, drugging her with his kiss. He tasted of pine and the outdoors, heat and man. He felt warm and hard against her, making her yearn in all her secret places. Yet the kiss, passionate as it was, still held back the full fire of him, the full passion she sensed lay just beneath his surface.

"*Zvyozdochka*," he whispered against her throat when he finally released her lips. "Be sure. For once I've had you, I may never want to let go."

If anything, his words only increased her desire. Keeping Peter in her life—possibly forever—was looking more and more attractive. No other man, not even any of the other bears in Grizzly Cove, had ever affected her this way. Peter was something special. Something she wanted to grab on to and keep.

"I'm sure," she whispered back. The two words were about all she could manage, though she was thinking that if, after tonight, he tried to run away from her, he'd learn just how well a *strega* could hunt.

Her words seemed to unleash the beast inside him, in the most delightful way. Peter growled deep in his throat. She could feel the sound reverberate from his chest through to hers wherever she pressed against him. The vibrations warmed her and made her want to make him growl again. Soon.

He bent to place both of his hands under her rump and lift. She helped, wrapping her legs around him as he began to walk farther into the apartment. She hoped he was heading for her bedroom, but instead, he paused at the kitchen island, seating her on the cold granite while his lips sought hers again.

His kiss was fire this time. Pure flame that burned her senses and made her want to bask. He was amazing. No more tentative touches and seducing kisses. No, this was the real deal. His passion had been unleashed, and his touch had turned from seducing to beguiling. She was completely in his thrall. Whatever he wanted to do—wherever he wanted to take her—she was a willing and eager participant.

Right about that time, she realized he'd been undressing her all the time he'd been kissing her. Her top was gone, and she felt his hands working at her bottoms, as well. The fabric left behind on the countertop acted as a buffer against the coolness of the stone beneath her, while his hands and mouth set fire to her skin wherever he touched or kissed.

His lips left hers to take a tour around her body. By the time he reached the sensitive tips of her breasts, she was moaning aloud. She heard rather than saw his response. A low, vibrating sound of appreciation rumbled from him. It was akin to a purr, but he was a bear inside, so she wasn't quite sure what to call it. Whatever it was, it was sexy as hell, and she wanted to hear it again. Preferably while he was inside her. Which couldn't happen soon enough for Mellie.

She helped him shuck her pants and let them drop to the floor. He caught her in his arms and didn't allow her to sit back down on the countertop until he'd put his shirt beneath her bare bottom. She'd been unbuttoning him all the while, so it was a simple matter for him to shrug out of the shirt on one side then, holding her against him with the free arm, use his other hand to arrange the shirt on the smooth counter.

When he set her back down on the edge of the granite slab, he reclaimed his place between her legs, the shirt under her allowing him to easily slide her closer so that she was open to him. But he still wore his jeans. The denim was rough against her inner thighs, but it felt so good. The only thing that would be better would be if she could feel his bare skin.

Putting actions to thoughts, Mellie reached for his belt buckle, fiddling with the mechanism to get it to release. Coming to her rescue, Peter took over the job, removing his jeans in a quick, decisive move that indicated to her he was as hot for this as she was. Good. She didn't want to wait.

Mellie wrapped her legs around him loosely as he stepped back to her, and…oh, yeah…she was right up against him. She could feel his eager hardness as it pressed close to the spot where she wanted it most. Mellie looked down and the sight made her breath catch as her excitement rose higher. He was magnificent. He was big and bold and ready. Heaven knew she was ready, too.

"Don't make me wait," she pleaded in a rough whisper that seemed to break the tension. He'd been holding back, but it was as if her words had freed him.

Peter aligned himself, pushing tentatively at first. She watched every move along with him. It was the most erotic thing she'd ever done, and it set this experience far above any other she'd ever had—and they hadn't even really started yet. She wasn't sure she'd survive Peter's lovemaking without her mind being completely blown if this was any indication.

He pushed, and she accepted. When he realized she was more than ready for him, he slid in confidently, in one smooth move that made her gasp. He was big, and she wasn't all that experienced. Especially lately. It had been a while since she'd done this, but her body was accommodating him even as the thought crossed her mind. *Mmm. Yeah.* That felt so incredibly good.

He tugged her closer, and she tore her gaze from the place where they'd joined to look deep into his eyes. Energy swirled in them, just below the surface. His bear was looking out at her from within his human gaze. She read satisfaction and possession. Dominance and…care? Oh.

Her heart shattered and reformed with a little piece of him inside. Peter had changed her in that moment, she knew. She would never be the same after this, but that wasn't necessarily a bad or scary thing. It felt right. *He* felt right.

And then, he began to move.

Rough, smooth, fast, slow. She wasn't sure what to expect with Peter, and he gave it all to her. All…and more. He seemed to know exactly how to touch her, how to move, how best to please her in every way. He was passionate and considerate at the same time. He took all she could give and gave back even more.

When her first climax hit, he was there, holding her as she shook in his arms, speaking words she didn't understand, whispering to her in Russian. Mellie thought absently that she was going to have to learn some Russian if they kept this up because she really wanted to know what he was saying.

She reached a second peak and then a third before Peter joined her. They came together as if they had done this a million times before, and with the way she felt for long, long moments after, she really looked forward to doing it again. Soon.

Apparently, so did Peter, because he lifted her off the counter and walked with her in his arms to her bedroom. Once there, he laid her on the bed as if she were made of spun glass, then came down beside her. Their gazed locked, and he began stroking her arm with one finger. A light touch that sent her recently sated senses spinning toward arousal once more, though she hadn't thought such a thing was possible after so short a time.

"You're amazing, *zvyozdochka*," he told her in a sleepy, sexy voice.

"*Zvyozdochka*," she repeated, trying to get the pronunciation right. "What does that mean?"

He raised his hand to push a strand of hair back from her face. "Little star," he translated. "It's how I think of you. Your magic shines so bright. Like a star."

"That's beautiful," she whispered, falling easily under his

spell once more. He leaned in to kiss her, and she went willingly, following him as he rolled onto his back so that she was over him this time.

If she thought being on top meant she'd be in control, Peter was quick to show her how deliciously wrong she was. With his enormous strength, he moved her around just the way he wanted her, bringing her hips over his and coaxing her down on top of him.

Unbelievably, he was as ready for more as she was. Maybe the Baker sisters hadn't been exaggerating when they'd been gossiping about how ready-for-anything their new husbands always were.

"Okay?" Peter asked, catching her eye. The sincere concern for her on his face touched her deeply.

"If I weren't, I would let you know," she assured him. "I've liked everything so far," she went on, enjoying the feel of him sliding inside her once more.

And then, she couldn't speak while he maneuvered her into motion. His big hands on her hips guided, but she did have some control over the speed and depth. She altered both at random with the idea of teasing him but only succeeded in driving herself crazy in the best possible way. At one point, as she shuddered in ecstasy, Peter took control of her hips, holding her to him as she came apart around him.

When she met his eye, he was clearly amused. His smile spoke of pure male satisfaction and pride. She couldn't really fault him for that. Being with him had brought her more pleasure than she could ever remember having. And it wasn't over yet.

She came again before he finally joined her, and then, miracle of miracles, he cuddled her into his arms, and she drifted, warm in his embrace. If she let herself, she might almost think he…cared for her? Maybe even loved her.

Wow. The L-word.

She was very much afraid she'd fallen head over heels with the big Russian teddy bear. Shoving thoughts of the future aside, she promised herself she would enjoy these moments, right now, in his arms. Tomorrow would take care of itself.

CHAPTER EIGHT

The next day dawned bright and clear. Mellie was alone in bed, but she knew at once that she wasn't alone in the apartment. Delicious breakfast smells were wafting down the hallway, and she could hear Peter's heavy footsteps as he moved around in the kitchen.

The thought brought a smile to her face. He was making noise on purpose, so she would know he was here. He had to be. She'd lived in Grizzly Cove long enough to know how silent the guys who lived here were, as a matter of course.

She was just coming out of the bathroom and planned to go join Peter in the kitchen when her phone rang. It was the special tone that told her Nonna was on the other end of the line.

She answered it eagerly, hoping there had been some progress on their dragon search. Sure enough, Nonna had called her friends in Italy and had some news to share.

"Rumors say there was a dragon in Venice for a while, but he moved on. One of my Venetian friends gave me the number for a priestess in the States who is mated to a werewolf with ties to a small Pack in the Canadian wilderness.

It's all very round-about, but she said to try this and call back if I don't get anywhere. Between you and me, she doesn't expect me to have to call back. Now, the question is, do I call the priestess or do you?" Nonna went on, not giving Mellie time to respond. "This is your quest, so it is best that you take it from here, I think."

She proceeded to give Mellie the contact information and number.

"Now, go back to your bear. Tell him I expect to meet him soon." Nonna hung up before Mellie had stopped stuttering. Nonna *knew*!

How embarrassing. Not that Mellie had spent the night with Peter, but that her grandmother—who had raised her with very high standards about who she let into her life and especially into her bed—had known. Mellie wondered if Urse was the recipient of Nonna's teasing, too, or if that was reserved for the sister who was still single.

Either way, Mellie wasn't about to waste any more time worrying about it right now. She had breakfast to eat and a dragon to track down. Both things she could accomplish with the help of the very scary, very potent, very lovable bear shifter, who was still waiting for her in the kitchen.

Peter heard when Mellie started moving around the other end of the apartment. He was content to give her some time to get herself together before they shared the meal he was preparing. Then, he heard her phone ring and listened to her side of the conversation. Good as his hearing was, he couldn't make out the other end with Mellie and the phone so far away. Still, it sounded as if she was talking to her grandmother, which meant their hunt might begin anew today.

Mellie came into the kitchen, a look of triumph on her face. "Nonna and her contact in Italy came through," she told Peter, coming right up to him to give him a delicious kiss hello before moving off toward the cooked bacon he had draining on a plate on the counter.

He followed, claiming her lips for a deeper kiss after she'd had her strip of crunchy bacon. There was nothing like bacon-flavored kisses from the woman he loved.

Yeah, that's right. Loved.

He'd come to terms with that concept in the middle of the night when his bear was making demands on his human half. Demands that they figure out a way to keep Mellie with them forever. Demands that made it clear the bear half wanted her in his den. For always.

The human half felt her in his heart and knew. Just like that. He loved her.

But humans were tricky. He wasn't sure how to tell her without scaring her off.

He couldn't be sure—seeing as how she wasn't a shifter—that she was on the same page. He'd have to be cautious and bide his time. He had to pick the right moment to tell her and hope she felt the same way.

He let the kiss end, unwilling to burn the first breakfast he'd ever made for his mate. He let her go with reluctance and turned back to the stove.

"What did your grandmother tell you?" Peter asked as he expertly flipped pancakes and plated eggs that were perfectly cooked—as long as you liked them well done.

When he turned back around, Mellie was holding up a slip of paper in one hand, waving it around with a happy grin. "She gave me the contact number for a priestess in the States. This priestess supposedly has ties to a small werewolf Pack out of Canada that might have news about the dragon."

It all sounded a bit tenuous to Peter, but he didn't say so. He didn't want to banish the happy look on Mellie's sweet face. Not when her grandmother had given her such hope.

"Do you want me to call?" he asked, unsure what she expected.

She seemed to think about it for a moment. "I think maybe I should call the priestess, but you should be on hand in case she needs to verify anything with a shifter. Then, if we get to the next step and get to talk to the werewolves, you should probably take the lead there."

Peter nodded. "It is a good plan. When do you want to do this?"

"Well, the priestess is on the east coast, so it's not too early to call her right now," Mellie offered. From the way she was hopping about, she was clearly too excited to wait. Peter shut down the stove and put all the food on the table before turning to her.

"Let's do this. Breakfast can wait for a few more minutes." His reward was her beaming smile.

She pulled out her phone and quickly began dialing. This time, with her standing no more than five feet away, he could hear everything. The phone rang, and the call was picked up on the other end. A woman said hello.

"Hi, is this Deena?" Mellie waited for the affirmative response before going on. "I'm Amelia Ricoletti. My grandmother got your number from a friend of hers in Italy. We are *strega*."

"*Strega*?" the woman on the other end repeated. "Why would a *strega* be calling me?"

Peter noticed that the woman seemed to know exactly what the word meant.

"It's somewhat complicated, but we need some information. Let me explain our situation, and then, perhaps you'll understand." Mellie told the woman about moving to Grizzly Cove and the sea monster problem she was trying to solve.

Mellie talked about the old grimoire and the need for dragon's blood. What she didn't mention was the bear population in Grizzly Cove. At least, she didn't say as much as she could have. Peter was pleased that Mellie shared only those secrets that were hers to share, holding back information that might prove dangerous to the others in town.

"My nonna said her contact thought that the dragon had moved to Canada and that you had some connection with a werewolf Pack up there. I'm really hoping that you might be able to put me in touch with the wolves so that I can pursue this lead," Mellie went on. "I give you my word of honor that I intend only to help in the fight against evil. I have no desire to harm the dragon, only ask him if he will aid me in my quest. If he refuses, I cannot and will not try to coerce him."

Silence fell as Mellie stopped speaking. Then, finally, the woman spoke.

"I've heard a little bit about Grizzly Cove. I know it's not common knowledge, and I would not spread rumors, but if the town is as I suspect, I'd need to talk to one of the…um…natives. The Canadians wouldn't welcome me introducing a *strega* into their midst, but if it's one of their own—or someone like them—I think it'll be easier. Plus, I'd like corroboration of your story before we go any further, no offense intended."

"None taken," Mellie said immediately. "I know this is all coming at you out of left field, and I respect your caution. I do have a friend here with me that might be able to set your mind more at ease. At the very least, he could put you in touch with someone who could vouch for me and my story. Would you like to talk to him?"

Receiving an affirmative answer, Mellie handed the phone to Peter. The priestess was cautious. Good. These were dangerous times they were all living in, and it paid to be cautious.

"Hello," Peter said, hoping his accent wasn't too thick for the woman to understand. "I am Peter Zilakov. I own the butcher shop and am also a part-time deputy," he told the priestess.

"I'm Deena." Immediately, Peter felt the woman's magic reaching through the phone to touch his. There was no doubt in his mind that this woman served the Goddess. Her power was pure and sparkling against his.

"It is an honor to make your acquaintance, milady," Peter told her. "Your power is…" Peter was almost lost for words, the energy was so pure. "It is almost divine, one might say," he told her honestly.

"You can feel that?" Deena sounded surprised.

"I'm a bear," he said, shrugging. "Some of us are more sensitive than others. And among shifters, we are some of the more magical."

"So I've heard, though I've never met one of your kind before. My mate is a wolf," she added, almost shyly.

"You are newly mated," Peter guessed. "Congratulations to you both."

"Thank you." Deena hesitated for a moment. "Would you mind talking to my mate? Perhaps you have friends in common or some other way to establish who you are. Unfortunately, I don't get out much and don't have a lot of friends in magical circles, though I've always heard most *strega* are good guys."

"I would be pleased to talk with your mate. As you can probably tell from my accent, I have been around the world a time or two and know a lot of people and places. I'm sure we can find some way of identifying exactly who we are, and I applaud your caution."

The priestess relinquished her phone to her mate and what followed was a detailed conversation where Peter and the other man—a werewolf named Josh—finally established mutual friends who would vouch for them. They ended the call so Josh could check his contacts about Peter, with the agreement to call back once more trust had been established.

In the meantime, Peter and Mellie ate the breakfast he had prepared. When Mellie's phone rang again, Peter answered it. Sure enough, it was the werewolf. Josh gave Peter a phone number and a name, then cautioned him to be careful before hanging up.

Peter looked at Mellie in triumph. They were one step closer.

The call to the werewolf Pack's Alpha was a little trickier. Even with the introduction from Josh, who turned out to be the Alpha's grandson, the Canadian werewolf leader was very leery of imparting any information. It took a while, but eventually, Peter was able to establish a rapport with the

Canadian Alpha.

"There is a newcomer in the area," Tom Mahigan, the cagey Canadian Alpha, finally admitted, about ten minutes into the phone call. "A big Russian fellow. He came to see me when he moved in down the ridge. A courtesy call. Sounded a lot like you do, and his power was… Well, it was kind of…immense, is the only word I can think of. He wasn't any kind of shifter I've ever come across before, but he had our energy. He didn't read like fey or mage. He was a shifter all the way."

"He could be the one we're looking for," Peter told the wolf Alpha.

"I can go out to see him and ask if he'll speak to you, but I can't promise anything. It'll be up to him."

Peter had hoped for more but understood the Alpha's position. "Just tell him about our leviathan problem and the fact that his input would be minimal. We're not asking him to fight the thing, just to help out with a potion to drive it from our shores."

"What about the long-term solution?" Tom asked. "Someone's going to have to fight the thing eventually."

"We're already working on that," Peter informed him. "Many of us in town have connections in the military, especially in the secret units populated by our kind. We've already got specialists on the way, but they have to fulfill their commitments to Uncle Sam first. We've been assured that, as soon as they're free, their next stop is here to help with our sea monster problem."

"You believe these military shifters will be able to handle it?" Tom sounded skeptical.

"They aren't shifters," Peter revealed, figuring how much he could say without risking operational security. "They're specialists though, who, we've been assured, are the best men for the job."

"Well, I suppose you know what you're doing. Personally, my Pack has seen both the good and bad side of dealing with mages. I hope you're sure about the ones you're working with." Tom sounded strange, and Peter sensed a story there but was unwilling to pry.

"The *strega* I'm working with has been vetted at the highest levels and has family ties to our town," Peter assured the other man. "Bears aren't easily fooled by those with magic, since we have so much of our own. We also have a shaman in residence who keeps an eye on all the magic here. Plus, the *strega* sisters have already proven their commitment to the town and to ridding us of the leviathan and protecting our people."

"Then, you're luckier than we were when a mage came to our Pack. The damage caused by just one mage took twenty years to rectify." The Alpha's tone had gone bleak. "We're only just starting to get over it. And we're still hunting the mage. If you ever hear word of a man named Mathias Bolivar, you steer clear and give me a call." The wolf's tone brooked no argument, but Peter wasn't going to decline the wolf's request in any case. One good turn deserved another.

"I've never heard the name before, but I won't forget. I'll ask around a bit, and if I hear anything, I'll be sure to pass it along," Peter promised the other man.

"Much obliged," Tom said, his tone going back to something a bit friendlier. "I'll be in touch soon about the newcomer. If he agrees to talk to you, you'll hear directly from him. If not, I'll call and let you know."

"Thanks," Peter said, glad the fellow was being reasonable.

Peter ended the call and turned to Mellie, who was watching him with impatient eyes.

"Well?" she prodded.

"He's going to talk to a newcomer to his area this afternoon. If the man is willing to talk to us, he'll call us direct. If not, the wolf Alpha will call and let us know."

"So, either way, we're waiting for a call," Mellie summed up. "I think I'll go stir crazy if I have to wait all day for the phone to ring."

"Tell you what," Peter said, rising from the table and

taking their empty dishes to the sink. "Is your sister coming in this morning to open the store?"

"Yeah, today's her day to open," Mellie told him. "But she won't be here for another hour. As you know, we don't open that early."

"That's good. We can go for a walk, then. Get your mind off waiting. You'll have your phone with you in case they call, but it didn't sound to me like we'd be hearing back for a few hours." Peter rinsed the plates and put them in the dishwasher as if he'd done so a million times before.

He'd certainly made himself at home in her apartment, but Mellie didn't mind at all. She liked the way he'd pitched in and wasn't walking on eggshells. It made the whole morning-after thing a lot easier to deal with. His matter-of-factness eased her nerves in a way she hadn't expected but valued greatly.

"Go get your coat. I'll finish up here, and then, we'll get out and clear our heads," he encouraged her.

"I'll just leave a note for Urse, so she doesn't worry about where I am," Mellie said decisively as she rose from the table and helped a bit by bringing another dish to him at the sink. She rose up on tiptoe and kissed his cheek. "Thank you," she told him, trying to convey the depth of feeling over all that he'd done for her.

Words were inadequate, but he seemed to understand. He paused, turning to her and bending slightly to kiss her lips. "You're welcome," he replied in an intimate tone that wasn't as sexy as it was understanding. Although…everything Peter did was sexy.

Mellie toddled off to get her coat, a bit in a daze from the lingering kiss and the rapid-fire events of the morning. Their search for a dragon had just kicked into high gear, and they might have a positive answer within a few hours.

Mellie hadn't expected such fast movement after so many months of struggle trying to brew the perfect protective potion. It was all happening so fast.

Peter's idea of getting out for a while was a really good

one. Though Mellie was a homebody by nature, she enjoyed the occasional walk along the beach. She hadn't done that in far too long—first, because it had been dangerous to be down near the water until Urse had done her magic, and second, because Mellie didn't like walking alone.

Before, she'd always had Urse with her if she wanted to do something, but Urse was married now. Going alone just emphasized to Mellie that she couldn't really call on Urse anymore for the casual sister activities that they'd taken for granted before.

No, now, there was always John to consider. He was a possessive, protective bear shifter, and to be fair, they were still in their honeymoon phase. Mellie knew Urse didn't like to be away from John any more than he liked being parted from his new mate. They both did their jobs, but any free time was spent together. They'd done their best to do things with Mellie, including a standing dinner invitation that Mellie took them up on at least once a week, but it just wasn't the same.

Mellie was used to being with Urse all the time. Now, the apartment was very empty without her sister in it. And walks along the now-safe beach by herself? No, thanks.

Walking with Peter at her side, though… That was different. In fact, it made Mellie feel like a new woman. Happy. Joyful. Cherished.

That last one was something that being with her sister certainly didn't evoke. Mellie smiled as she slid her arm through Peter's as they walked slowly together down the early-morning beach. The sun was still low enough on the horizon to make her squint a bit. It was going to be a sunny day, for a change.

"Getting used to overcast all the time was one of the hardest things about moving here," Mellie told Peter, making small talk as they walked down the quiet beach. "I like rain, though, so I got used to it."

"This region is known for the constant rain and clouds, but the temperatures are very mild, so I see it as a trade off,"

Peter told her.

"What's it like where you grew up?" she asked, snuggling close to his side.

"Cold," he replied with a hint of humor. "Most of the time," he clarified. "But it's a beautiful place, Kamchatka. Rugged and few people. Many bears. Many shifters of different kinds. Lots of nature and the magic it makes."

"Sounds beautiful," she said, and they walked along farther down the beach.

About ten minutes later, Mellie's phone rang, and she jumped, fumbling in her pocket for the device. Surely, the werewolf hadn't found the dragon that quickly? Mellie looked at the screen, and all the tension drained out of her.

"It's my sister," she told Peter, punching the button to answer the call. "Hi, Urse. Did you get my note?"

"I got it," her sister replied, sounding very suspicious. "Where are you?"

"On the beach, taking a walk," Mellie replied, sticking to the truth.

"With Peter? Mellie, what's going on with you two?" Urse asked flat out, and Mellie stuttered.

Then, her phone beeped in her ear. She looked at the screen quickly and got back to her sister.

"I'm getting another call. I'll talk to you later. This could be really important." Without even waiting for her sister to say goodbye, Mellie hung up on her and connected the other call. It was from Canada. "Hello?"

"Amelia Ricoletti?" came the gruff voice of the werewolf Alpha.

"Yes. Alpha Mahigan?" Mellie looked up at Peter, her eyes going wide.

"You're in luck, young lady," the werewolf told her. "I ran into the Russian at the general store and took him aside to tell him about your call. He won't speak to you, but he wants the information for the Alpha in your area. He's a cautious fellow."

"Oh." Mellie felt a bit disappointed but still hopeful. "Let me give the phone to Peter. He can get you what you need." She held the phone against her chest and spoke to Peter. "He wants—"

"I heard," Peter told her gently and held his hand out for the phone. She relinquished it to him, grateful for shifter hearing that she didn't have to repeat everything.

Peter moved a short way off and exchanged words with the werewolf Alpha, reciting information for the other man before ending the call. He walked the short distance back to her and handed her the phone.

"We should talk to John," he told her with a slight frown. "I'm not sure if the dragon really will call John, or if this is some kind of delaying tactic, but he needs to know either way."

"I'll call Urse back. She'll know where John is," Mellie said, already punching the screen on her phone. "He doesn't always go right in to the office. Sometimes, he hangs around the store with my sister for a bit, or goes to check on some of the outliers. Either way, Urse is the fastest way to find him."

Urse picked up the phone in a bit of a temper at having been cut off before, but Mellie didn't have time to waste placating her sister. "Where's John?" Mellie asked over her sister's annoyance.

"Why?" Urse immediately shut down the mini-tirade about being hung up on and switched tacks. "What's wrong?"

"Nothing, but we need to talk to him right away," Mellie told her sister.

"We?" Urse's voice took on a suspicious tone. "You're with Peter, aren't you?"

Mellie sighed. "Yeah. I am. But that doesn't change the fact that we need to find John."

"No, you don't," Urse said, amusement in her voice now. "He's here. He's fixing that leaky sink in the downstairs bathroom."

"Good," Mellie said with relief. "Don't let him leave. We're coming right back."

Mellie hung up on her sister for the second time that day

and pocketed her phone as she turned back toward the direction of the bookstore. She glanced up at Peter to fill him in, but he was smiling.

"I heard," he told her as they took off at a much brisker pace than that which they'd set out with on the way to this spot. They were about halfway around the cove, but Mellie was confident John would stay put at the store until they got there.

John was understanding and even encouraging when he heard what Peter and Mellie had been up to. Urse gave Mellie a knowing look but didn't tease her as badly as Mellie had feared, even after Peter and John left. Peter had to see to his grandmother before opening his store, and John always had mayor stuff to do.

The bookshop was busier than usual, with a shipment having been delivered two days ago. Everyone in town knew when the deliveries were made, since the truck came through only rarely. They were polite enough to give the sisters time to sort everything out, but then, those who had special ordered particular volumes would show up, looking for their books.

Urse stayed for most of the afternoon, the sisters sharing a quick lunch Urse picked up at the bakery down the street, while they continued to sort through the big boxes of stock that had been delivered for the store. Thankfully, Urse laid off the teasing, and Mellie was able to keep her delicious memories of the night before to herself for a while. She didn't exactly daydream, but Urse caught her staring into space at least once, though she didn't make a big fuss over it, for which Mellie was grateful.

Peter called after Urse left for the night to say he would try to stop by during his patrol, but he was working the night shift on his part-time gig as a deputy sheriff. She knew he wouldn't be able to stay long. The duty of protecting the cove and its residents was something he took very seriously, but it would be good to at least say hello and maybe share a cup of coffee on his break. Mellie told him she'd be waiting.

CHAPTER NINE

The dragon winged in under cover of darkness. Peter felt the weight of the dragon's presence in the sky above, though he'd never felt such a thing before and couldn't see anything in the pitch-black night. He just knew.

He'd left Mellie hours before, sorry he couldn't spend time with her tonight, but perhaps it had worked out for the best. Being on patrol—awake in the wee hours of the night when everyone else in town was either going about their business or fast asleep—meant that Peter was hyper-aware of any threats that might come in the night. He wasn't sure if the dragon was a threat, exactly, or not, but it was definitely something dangerous and an unknown quantity.

So far, the energy felt more curious than damning. The dragon seemed to be flying around, pausing here or there. If anything, Peter would surmise that the shifter was checking out the town before he made contact.

One point in the man's favor—the ward around the town had let him past without raising any alarms. From what Peter had heard, evil would never be able to pass Urse's wards without a major production. If Peter hadn't been watching so carefully, he doubted he would even have noticed the dragon's entrance. Which meant he wasn't evil. A good thing.

Whether or not he would help them remained to be seen.

*

The dragon sensed great magic at work in the tiny town below. Evidence of building projects was easily seen, as were the signs of habitation. From above, he also sensed magic in the waters of the cove. Interesting.

Paul was familiar with bears and the intense flavor of their magic, but the sea creatures in the cove were elusive. Not so the evil pulsating from just off shore. So. They weren't kidding when they said they had a sea monster problem.

Paul winged over the potent magical barrier that blocked the cove from the rest of the ocean, noting the interest of the tentacled beasts beyond. They sensed him. Not good.

He made for a likely tree that would support his weight. A giant sequoia, if he wasn't mistaken. Now, this was a *tree*. He liked the Pacific Northwest already, though he'd never been here before. They had trees that could truly hold a dragon and even hide him from below. Nice.

From his perch high atop the massive tree, Paul took note of the town again. He saw the heat signatures of beings in slumber, and a few on the prowl. One was watching the skies, and if his eyesight wasn't failing him, that one wore a uniform with a shiny bright star on his chest. A policeman of some kind. And he seemed aware of something amiss. Good instincts.

Paul didn't know what to make of a town that concentrated so many bear shifters in one place. Even more confusing was that they seemed to be in league with powerful *strega*. It was somewhat unprecedented, though in ancient times, he'd read that shifters often coexisted alongside mages and other magical folk, banding together to fight evil.

Rumors abounded about the return of Elspeth, the so-called Destroyer. Paul was young. He hadn't been around the last time Light had fought Dark and succeeded. Frankly, he didn't know what to make of the strange happenings in recent years, only that something was happening. Something not good.

Paul had thought long and hard about which side he would take if the battle came to a head in his lifetime. He hadn't completely decided one way or the other until very recently.

His life hadn't been easy to this point, and he'd never really benefited from being good. He hadn't really tried being completely bad either. He honestly wasn't sure he had it in him. There was still a fragile human heart inside his dangerous beast body. That heart had been battered and bloodied, but it still beat with compassion for the underdog and yearned to protect those weaker than himself.

Which was basically everybody. Though, they didn't know it. Paul flew under the radar as much as possible and spent most of his time now traveling the world, chasing rumors of other dragons. More than anything, he wanted to find others of his kind. There had to be more dragons. Somewhere.

He just hadn't found any yet. That didn't mean he wouldn't keep trying. He had to have come from somewhere. Finding out what had happened to his family was important to him, but even just finding another dragon somewhere on Earth would be a big deal to a man who had grown up an orphan.

Luckily, his dragon form had come to him in adulthood. He'd already been living on his own, far out of town when his first change had come upon him. He hated to think what could have happened to him otherwise. Living all his childhood in one of those notorious Romanian orphanages where the babies were never held had left him scarred…but not broken.

He'd fought for every step he'd taken on the path to a normal life until he was eighteen and living on the side of a mountain. Then, the dragon had come to him, and everything had changed. Suddenly, he had way more questions about his origins than he'd had before and another line of inquiry, though finding out about secretive shifters wasn't an easy thing. Especially when other shifters recognized him as one of their kind but couldn't place his animal.

He often got by claiming he was some sort of bear, but that wouldn't work here in Grizzly Cove. Besides, they already knew about him. In this place, he would wear his own skin and his true identity. It was a novel concept.

Settling in the massive tree to wait for dawn, Paul decided he'd meet the *strega* and her bear friend then decide what to do from there. He could always fly away. Even a Clan of bears would be no match for his dragon. Though that thing in the water…

Paul looked out over the ocean and saw what looked like massive tentacles sticking up out of the water against the dark horizon. That thing was a beast. He wondered, if his dragon took on the leviathan, which one would come out the victor.

*

Mellie yawned as she turned the sign on the bookshop's door from CLOSED to OPEN. She hadn't gotten a lot of sleep last night. Currents of magic had swirled around her, making her restless all night long. She thought maybe it had been her imagination, but there was something different about the energy of the town today. Something…not quite normal.

Not that Grizzly Cove had ever been *normal*, per se. She smiled to herself at the thought. Get a town full of highly magical shifters, and things were bound to be a little different.

She went back to the desk and sat down, just enjoying the morning for a moment before she started in on the work that was waiting for her. Peter had worked the night shift, so she wasn't sure when she'd be seeing him, though there was a good chance he'd stop in before he went off shift this morning. She knew that the night shift guy usually stuck around for a debrief before the day shift guy clocked on, so they should be doing that right around now.

She sipped her coffee and looked through the open doorway to the backroom. There were still a couple of boxes that needed unpacking, and then, she could work on the front window display.

The bell rang above the door, and she turned, expecting to see Peter, but the smile froze on her lips as her gaze met that of a total stranger. A very big, very scary, total stranger.

In a town full of big, scary men, this guy was in a class all by himself. Mellie swallowed her fear and thought about her options should this guy become violent. She was a *strega.* A powerful hereditary witch. There had to be something she could do if the worst should happen, right?

If she had the right potion, she could turn the guy into a frog, but all her good brews were upstairs. Not that she had ever brewed up anything that would turn anybody into anything even remotely resembling a frog…

She was babbling, even in her own mind. *Get a grip, Mel!*

"Be at ease, little one. I have come, as requested, to listen to your plea."

His voice was like waves rippling on lava. Fire and brimstone and the rumbles of the earth. For a moment, she was mesmerized by the sheer power of his voice.

"What?" Mellie blinked, breaking the spell and retreated behind the counter, putting some space between herself and this beguiling man. "Who are you, and what do you want?"

"It is more a question of what you want from me. To answer your first question, I am the dragon."

"Holy shit." The profanity left her mouth in a stunned whisper, and thankfully, the dragon-man thought it was funny. He laughed while she tried to regain her wits. "I— I'm sorry. I'm Mellie Ricoletti. Thank you for coming. To be honest, I was only expecting a phone call where I could plead for your help."

The suave dragon shifter gestured toward himself smoothly. "And yet, here I am. You can make your plea in person. I have already seen what you are up against in the ocean." For the first time, he seemed unsure, and Mellie was glad. That little bit of uncertainty made him seem more human.

"The leviathan," Mellie confirmed. "And a few hundred of its minions. Or maybe a few thousand. There's no way to be really sure."

"Why has it come here? Do you have any theories?" The dragon shifter moved closer, but the sturdy counter was still between them, and for now, Mellie wasn't any more afraid of the guy than she had been a moment ago, so she was holding her own.

"The concentration of magical energy is what my nonna and her friends believe brought it here. There were rumors of it off the coast of Italy and in other parts of the world earlier, then one day, it showed up here. It tried to eat the Master Vampire of Seattle. It crunched on his yacht when he was doing reconnaissance on the town and ate his crew. He made it ashore but was badly damaged. He has since formed a strategic alliance with the bears here."

"You don't say? That is an odd occurrence, indeed." The dragon released her from his gaze as he looked out the window toward the water across the street. "And what of the creatures in the cove itself? What are they?"

He would find out sooner or later, and he already knew something was there in the water, so Mellie figured it couldn't hurt anything to enlighten him. Lying to this man wasn't likely to earn his trust or help with her potion.

"A pod of mer were attacked by the leviathan and its minions. The Alpha bear offered them sanctuary, and my sister cast permanent wards to safeguard the waters of the cove."

"Your sister?" the dragon looked back at her, capturing her gaze once more. "Blood kin or merely another *strega*?" he asked.

"There's nothing *mere* about being *strega*," she replied a bit haughtily. Who did this guy think he was to talk down to her?

He blinked in a way that wasn't quite human. It was like he had two eyelids or something. Like a lizard.

Oh, yeah. He was a dragon. *Shit.*

"To answer your question, Urse is my older sister. Blood

kin, as you call it. And she's now mated to the Alpha bear." Mellie added that to quell the interest she thought she saw in the dragon shifter's eyes.

"I have seen her ward. It seems your sister is truly a power. I wonder if you are the same?" He advanced another step, but Mellie held firm.

"We have different gifts." She could at least say that without giving too much away. "Urse does spells. I do potions."

"And it is for a potion that you seek a dragon?" he asked, one eyebrow rising in question.

"Yes. I've been given the task of creating a potion that will push the leviathan and its minions even farther out to sea. As my sister protected the cove, I aim to protect the coast." She'd never come out and stated her goal to anyone—not even Urse—but Mellie knew that, if she could just come up with the right potion, she could protect most of the Pacific coast of North America…given enough time for the potion to disperse.

"Ambitious," the dragon shifter commented. "But can you really do it?"

"My sister casts permanent wards. My grandmother sees the future. It was Nonna who set us on these tasks. So far, we're doing pretty well. Urse batted hers out of the ballpark. Now, it's my turn." Mellie might have put a bit too much bravado into her words, but she was on shaky footing with this oppressively dominant male.

"And you need my help to complete your task," the dragon shifter stated. "Tell me, what brought you to this conclusion? You have a lot of powerful beings here. Surely, one of them could help you instead."

"I've tried just about everything I could think of," Mellie admitted. "The potion recipe I'm following comes from an ancient grimoire."

"You didn't dream up the recipe yourself?" The dragon shifter seemed surprised…and impressed?

"Not for something this important. Not yet. I'm a good

potion witch, but it'll take a lifetime to get to the point where I can craft a potion of this magnitude from scratch. If I get to that point, I will add to the Ricoletti grimoire, but only after a lifetime's study and practice. I'm only in my twenties. Give a girl a break." She smiled slightly to soften her words, and the man seemed to respond to her friendliness. He shrugged.

"I'm young for a dragon, too. There are many lessons still to learn, I suppose. I hadn't thought about how it must work for a mage." He refocused his attention on her. "So, you've been given access to an ancient book of spells, and you picked one that called for a dragon?"

"Something like that. Actually, the way the book works, it will only show me the page I need. I can't open it to any other page. It reveals its knowledge only when truly necessary, so the fact that it showed me exactly one, and only one, recipe means that's the only shot I've got at getting this right." Mellie warmed to her subject. "I tried other magical and mundane creatures to substitute for the dragon ingredient, but nothing worked on the scale we all need this to work. Frankly, I didn't believe dragons existed, and I figured the word had been used as a euphemism until I spoke to Peter and his grandmother."

"Peter. This is your bear friend?" the man asked.

"Peter is…everything," she admitted, knowing she had to be totally honest. She saw the glimmer of interest in those alien-lizard eyes, and she didn't want him getting any ideas. She noted his comprehension and a fleeting look of disappointment as he nodded. "Peter's grandmother is visiting from Russia. They are Kamchatka bears, but I recently learned they had a dragon ancestor. Until I found that out, I thought dragons were either a fairytale or they'd died out long ago."

The dragon shifter's gaze grew intense. "They have dragon blood?" he asked, his tone holding deep interest. "Are you sure?"

"I tried the spell with Peter's help, and we actually got a good result that time. It wasn't as potent as it needs to be, but the potion did drive some of the smaller creatures away from the shore up by the stone circle."

"I saw the circle from the air. A new formation," the dragon observed almost absently. "Great magic is at work here. I'm not certain I should add mine to it, but I would like to talk to both your Peter and his grandmother, if you can arrange it."

Mellie caught sight of something through the glass door of the shop, and she smiled. "That won't be too hard to arrange. Peter's here."

Peter didn't like the way the stranger was looming over Mellie. He entered the store and was immediately hit by a wave of the other shifter's dominance. He was a scary mofo, as the Americans would say, but Peter was Kamchatka. There was little in the world that he could not handle.

He realized immediately that this must be the presence he had felt last night. He approached openly, sending a glance toward Mellie to make sure she was all right. She was smiling at him. His brave mate was not cowed by the dominance of the men in her little store. On the contrary, she was sure of her own power and place in the world. She would not be cowed either.

Brave mate. Perfect mate.

And, yes, he admitted. She was most definitely his mate... Whether she realized that or not was still an open question. Though, hopefully, not for long.

"Welcome to Grizzly Cove," Peter began, talking directly to the other man and trying to sound friendly. "I am Peter Zilakov."

"Paul Lebchenko," the other man said, surprising Peter with his candor. "Are you the bear with dragon blood?" he asked boldly. Peter shot a look at Mellie, surprised that she would have shared such an important secret with a stranger. Even if he was a dragon.

"It is not something we talk about openly," Peter replied. "Dragons have long been hunted, and my ancestor sought our Clan as sanctuary and was said to be relieved when all of his children proved to be bears and not dragons."

"You bastard!" Mellie surprised Peter with her vehemence, and he realized it was directed at the dragon shifter. "You used some sort of coercion charm on me, didn't you? That's just…low."

"I needed information, and you had it," Paul shrugged as if it didn't matter. Peter frowned.

"That sort of thing isn't done here, friend," he warned the man, a growl he couldn't contain rumbling in his throat. How dare this guy use any sort of magic against Mellie?

"I'm sorry, Peter," Mellie said, coming to his side and taking his arm. She was presenting them as a united force against the dragon, which made the bear in him settle down a bit. "I never would have betrayed your confidences willingly."

"I know, *zvyozdochka*." He petted her arm soothingly but kept wary eyes on the other man. "Look, buddy," Peter directed his words to Paul. "No matter how much we might need your help, there are rules here, in our territory. If you won't adhere to them, you can leave."

Paul bowed his head slightly. "I have been duly warned. But don't worry. The wards on this building, and the town as a whole, would not have let me use any truly harmful magic on anyone here. The fact that your lady was so free with her words means that the time for secrets—at least that one—is over. The charm I used is not magic in the earthly sense, but something gifted by the Lady of Light."

"You serve the Goddess?" Mellie's tone was disbelieving but also a bit curious.

"The Mother of All and I have had a rocky relationship in the past, but we're on good terms now," the dragon said, shocking them. He spoke of the Goddess as if She was just another person. Not the all-powerful force for good in the universe. "She and I have an understanding. I am looking for other dragons. She allows me certain…liberties in the hunt."

"Like using magic on someone with so many wards on her and her home that any normal spell wouldn't penetrate?"

Peter countered.

Paul bowed his head in acknowledgment. "Something like that. As of this moment, you are the closest thing I've ever come to finding one of my kin," he went on to say, further surprising Peter. "I would very much like to know more about your ancestor."

"You have no family of your own?" Mellie of the soft heart asked.

"I was raised—if that's what you could call it—in a Romanian orphanage under the regime of Nicolae Ceausescu. I have no idea where I came from or who my people are, though I've been looking for quite a while." He turned his gaze to Peter. "I wasn't kidding when I said you're the closest thing to family I've ever found. Your lady said something about your grandmother?"

"She is visiting," Peter admitted. "I believe she will talk with you about her grandfather, if you're not too obnoxious about it. Try any magic on her, and she'll box your ears, dragon or not."

Paul laughed out loud at that. "I think I will enjoy meeting your grandmother," he said at last.

"First, though, there's the little matter of my potion," Mellie reminded them all. Then, she seemed to realize how that sounded, and she backpedaled. "Not that I would make meeting Granny Ivana conditional on your helping with my task. Far from it. If you decide to help me, it has to be completely of your own volition. I'm convinced that's the only way to brew the strongest possible potion for what I hope to do."

"And your goal is protecting the coastline from the leviathan?" Paul asked.

"The coast and all the people, animals and Others who live on or near it and need to use the coastal waters. Right now, we've just been lucky that the leviathan and its friends have been preoccupied up here and haven't ravaged farther down the shore where humans abound. There'd be no way to keep it under wraps if too many humans were attacked," she told him.

Peter was a bit surprised by the scope of the protection Mellie hoped to cast. He hadn't really thought too much about her ultimate goal. He'd just assumed she wanted to help keep the residents of Grizzly Cove safe, but Mellie had different plans. Big plans. Plans that were way off the scale of what he thought they'd be.

He felt pride swell his chest. She was a good woman, who wanted to help people she didn't even know all up and down the coast. He wondered if she'd be able to pull it off. Based on her sister's immense magical ability, Mellie just might do it.

Then, Peter wondered if John had any idea what the goal for Mellie's potion was. Mated to Urse, he probably knew more about it than anyone else but had wisely kept his own counsel. That way, whatever Mellie managed to do, nobody but a select few would know what she'd been aiming for and whether or not she'd fallen short of her goal.

Still, she was thinking big. Very big. Peter hoped she wouldn't be disappointed.

"After surveying the town and the creatures on the other side of the ward, I am leaning toward helping you, but I'd like some more time to consider. I'd also like to meet the Alpha who dreamed up this place," Paul told them, looking from Mellie to Peter.

"That can be arranged. In fact, I'm pretty sure John would want to meet you before we go any further anyway. I briefed him this morning when I clocked off about your arrival last night," Peter told him, glad to see a little bit of surprise and perhaps respect enter the dragon's eyes.

"You are a policeman?" Paul asked. "I saw a man with a badge scanning the skies last night. That was you."

Peter nodded. "I'm a part-time deputy sheriff. The rest of the time, I own the butcher shop." Peter followed Mellie's gaze out the window of the bookstore and smiled. "You're about to get your wish. Here comes our Alpha and his mate. You can meet them right now."

CHAPTER TEN

Mellie was relieved to see Urse and John making their way to the bookstore. Urse had to have known when the dragon used magic within one of her wards. Thank goodness she'd thought to bring John with her when she came to investigate. Sometimes, it was really handy to have the Alpha bear as brother-in-law.

Mellie wasn't sure what to make of the dragon shifter. Was he a good guy or a bad one? She didn't know what to think. It was rude in the extreme to use magic against someone in their own home—a home that had been warded by one of the strongest witches of their generation against such things.

That he'd managed to do it anyway was troubling. That he claimed to have some special arrangement with the Goddess Herself was…astounding.

Then again, he was supposedly a dragon, for goodness sake. This was something totally outside Mellie's experience. She'd encountered several kinds of shifters and other magical folk, but dragons were a thing of legend only. She had no idea what to expect, and she doubted anyone in town—aside from Peter and his babushka—had any knowledge at all about honest-to-goodness dragon shifters.

Mellie was glad to let Peter take the lead in introducing John. Urse came directly around the counter to stand by Mellie's side, asking with a quick look if she was okay. Mellie nodded slightly, glad of her sister's support but really interested in what would happen next among the trio of men whose mere presence was filling the bookstore.

Bears had a big magical footprint, but the dragon was off the charts. Containing all three of them within the confines of the bookstore might be all right on the physical plane, but on the magical plane, the place was close to capacity. Of course, Urse's wards were so good, they'd stretch to accommodate whatever two *strega*, two bears and one big-assed dragon presence could throw at them.

The men talked for a few minutes, establishing who they were and who they knew in common. John seemed skeptical, at first, but willing to hear the other man out, and he kept shooting glances at Urse, who stood next to Mellie.

"You okay?" Urse asked aloud once the men moved away to talk about military connections in low voices.

"Yeah. Peter was here almost immediately, but that dragon guy used a charm on me." Her tone indicated her indignation and shock.

"Nervy," Urse observed. "But I felt it through my wards. The minute he started using magic in here, I knew to come."

"Glad you brought John as backup," Mellie said quietly, their entire conversation taking place in very low tones. Mellie was pretty sure the shifters could still hear them if they wanted to listen in, but she figured they were busy enough talking about top-secret shifter stuff.

Not that there was much of that between Urse and her mate, but appearances had to be maintained. Mellie supposed there were lots of shifter things she and her sister knew nothing about, though now that Urse was mated to John, that would change, given time.

Mellie knew enough to guess that there was nothing John wouldn't share with his mate. And vice versa. Mellie envied them their relationship and wished she could find that kind of devotion with…well, with Peter.

Since meeting him, all other men had faded from view. Peter had taken over all her fantasies of happy ever after, even before they'd made love. Now, all she could think about was him and when they could be together again. She hoped he'd be able to come over tonight, since he was off-duty, but they hadn't had a chance to talk about their plans yet.

The men stepped back toward the counter, their top-secret confab apparently finished for now. Paul's gaze landed on Urse as he strode forward.

"I understand you are the talented *strega* who cast the permanent wards I was able to examine from aloft last night. You do very nice work, indeed," Paul said to Urse.

"Thank you." Urse was blushing, if Mellie wasn't mistaken.

Son of a gun. She hadn't seen her sister blush in a very long time. Mellie stepped back to observe for a moment, wanting to be certain that Paul wasn't using more magic on them. The stinker.

Luckily for Paul's sake, Mellie didn't detect any extraneous magic. It had to be just the force of his enormous presence having its natural effect. Mellie found it somewhat difficult to be confined in this small room with such big magical personalities. Nothing in her life to date had prepared her for receiving a dragon through the door of her bookshop.

"We're going over to City Hall," John told the sisters. "We still have a few things to discuss with our guest. A few I's to dot and T's to cross," John said offhandedly, though Mellie sensed there was much more to his words than he let on.

Mellie was relieved. She needed a break from all the testosterone and intense magical presences. She would gird herself mentally for the next encounter with the dragon—if there was going to be one. She really hoped so. She still needed his help.

"I will be back," Paul promised her, his dragon eyes catching and holding hers, making her feel almost as if she was under some sort of spell. "I will not leave without giving you my answer regarding your potion."

"Thank you," Mellie breathed as Paul looked away, releasing her from his regard.

The three men swept from the bookshop, leaving the sisters behind. Peter sent a lingering glance over his shoulder before following behind the other two, but he didn't say anything. Mellie wished she could've had just a moment to hug him, but events were moving too quickly to accommodate her fear and tender sensibilities. Still, he'd seemed concerned when he looked back at her, which was enough for now. She'd get all the hugs of reassurance she needed tonight—if she had anything to say about it.

"Whew!" Urse let out a harsh breath and sort of collapsed against the countertop as the door shut behind the trio of powerful shifters. "That was intense."

"You can say that again," Mellie agreed, also loosening her stance. She hadn't realized how tense she had been holding herself until she tried to relax her shoulders. "Ouch." Mellie's right hand went up to her neck, rubbing out the pain caused by stiff muscles.

"Now, tell me, what the heck was that all about?" Urse asked, turning toward her sister.

"Oh, the dragon, you mean?" Mellie couldn't be absolutely certain, but she had a feeling John either hadn't wanted, or hadn't had a chance, to tell Urse about Peter's morning debrief about the arrival of an honest-to-goodness real live dragon shifter in Grizzly Cove overnight.

"Dragon?" Urse repeated, confirming Mellie's suspicions. "What do you mean, *dragon*? They're extinct." Urse gave Mellie a disbelieving look. "Aren't they?"

Now, it was Mellie's turn to finally come clean about all the stuff she hadn't told her sister over the past couple of days. She wouldn't tell Urse *everything*. The relationship with Peter was too new to talk about just yet. But she could definitely use Urse's advice and thoughts about the magical stuff relating to the potion she was trying to brew.

Starting from the last failure with the komodo dragon, Mellie filled Urse in. She glossed over Urse's pointed looks when Mellie talked about meeting Peter's grandmother. The fact that dragon shifters once existed, and still did, was enough to sidetrack Urse from any further questions about Peter. At least for the moment.

When Mellie talked about the series of phone calls that culminated in the dragon shifter's appearance in Grizzly Cove, Urse seemed to be stunned. She didn't say anything for a long moment and got the look on her face that Mellie always associated with Urse checking her magical wards. Then, Urse was back, her expression bemused, her head shaking as if she still couldn't quite believe what Mellie had just told her.

"There was a freaking *dragon* shifter in our shop just now?" Urse asked, apparently still in need of clarification—or perhaps, confirmation.

Mellie nodded. "Yup. He's a dragon. Peter said something about noting the presence of the dragon flying overhead last night, and Paul said he saw Peter watching him. He also said he'd taken an aerial tour of the town, and your wards, under cover of darkness, but he hadn't quite figured out what kind of magical creatures were living in the cove. I think that's when he started to put the whammy on me, using some sort of coercive charm to get me to spill my guts about every little thing. I told him about the mer. I even told him about Peter's family—which was something I'd promised not to tell anyone."

"Wait. What about Peter's family?" Urse asked quickly.

"Shit. Forget I said that. It's nothing bad, I promise. All you need to know is that his grandmother had the right contacts to connect us to this dragon guy, Paul." Mellie made a face and shook her head. "Is it possible the coercion charm is still active in here? I haven't been this bad at keeping secrets since I was three years old."

"Let me check again," Urse said, shutting her eyes this time as she ran through the magical strands of spells she had layered on the shop. "Hmm. It's an odd sort of spell, but it's dissipating now." Urse opened her eyes and looked at Mellie. "That was something I've never seen before, but it looked very useful for eliciting information. I wonder if I could recreate it?"

"Experiment later. For now, tell me how long until the charm is completely spent," Mellie groused.

"Well, let's put it this way. It's a good thing we don't keep much from each other, but I would suggest closing the shop for the rest of the day unless you want to start hearing some things you probably wouldn't want to know from our customers and probably telling them stuff you wouldn't want them to know about us."

"Enough said." Mellie went right over to the door and turned the sign. No way was she spilling any more secrets than she already had. Then, she turned back to Urse. "Does it extend to upstairs?" Then, she had a scary thought. "Is it cast on the place or is it on me, personally?" Mellie held her breath until her sister replied.

"It's on the shop, not on you. I think he wanted to generalize the effect so that anyone he talked to in here would be compelled to speak of things they normally wouldn't. Very, very clever," Urse mused, with an almost admiring light in her eyes.

"I think we'd better go upstairs. Not that I have all that many secrets from you, sis, but the guys might come back. I don't want them subject to that spell down here." Another thought occurred. "Will you notice if he does it again? What about down at John's office? Could he be using magic on them right now?"

"I'd know," Urse told her sister. "I have so many wards on this town right now that I know whenever out-of-the-ordinary magic is used."

"Really?" If what Urse was saying was true, that represented a huge step up from what she'd been doing before she mated with John.

Maybe the sisters were keeping more from each other than

ever before. Mellie felt hurt for a moment until she realized this was inevitable. They were growing apart as they found lives of their own with their chosen partners. Urse was doing stuff with John now and not consulting Mellie on every little thing. When Mellie mated—hopefully with Peter, if he would only agree—the same would likely hold true for her.

She tried not to be sad about it. It was a natural progression. It was part of growing up. They were still closer than most siblings. They would share their triumphs and tragedies. There would just be more people around them. More members of their family. More love to go around. So, it really was a positive thing, right?

"After I cast the permanent wards, John started asking me about less intensive uses of ward magic. We've been experimenting. In particular, I started to spell cast on his office and his work place almost right away. I don't want anything to happen to that man. Especially not something I can help prevent. If magic starts flying, I want to know about it."

"I can see that," Mellie allowed, not altogether surprised by the vehemence of her sister's words. When Urse loved, she loved fiercely, and she loved John as deeply as a woman could love a man. They were the real thing.

The sisters adjourned to the upper level apartment and worked side by side in the kitchen for a few minutes, making coffee and setting up snacks. Grizzly Cove men were always up for a snack, and when the guys returned, they would be ready.

"So… You and Peter?" Urse asked, carefully broaching the subject, even though she probably knew from Mellie's previous reaction that she didn't really want to talk about it.

"Yeah," Mellie admitted on a sigh. "But can we leave it at that for now? Please? It's still very new."

"I hear you," Urse said, cradling her hot mug of coffee in both hands and sitting back in her chair at the kitchen table. "Just… You know where I am if you ever want to talk about it. Loving a bear is kind of different than what we were raised to expect out of a relationship."

"I'm sure," Mellie rolled her eyes, knowing her sister would understand the gesture as a comment on the men, not on Urse's words. They both laughed.

Only a few minutes later, they both heard heavy feet clomping up the stairs to the apartment. John had a key to the shop, and he knew to make noise so as not to sneak up on the sisters. Could they be returning so soon? Mellie looked at Urse, and she was smiling. She knew exactly who had passed through her wards.

"It's John, Peter and the new guy," Urse said. "They're back."

Mellie stood to get mugs down from the cabinet as Urse went to unlock the door and let them in. Mellie poured coffee, feeling rather than seeing Peter come up behind her.

"You all right?" he asked in a low tone, for her ears only.

"I'm good. What about you?" she asked, turning to him.

The fire in his eyes made her breath catch. He was standing much closer than she had expected. She handed him a mug of coffee, to both give herself an excuse to touch him and to keep him at arm's length. She didn't feel like this was the appropriate time to go public with their relationship.

He growled deep in his throat. He didn't like being kept away, but he allowed it. For now. At least, that's the impression she got from the possessive look in his eyes. A little tingle flared through her. She couldn't wait until they were alone.

When they were all seated around the kitchen table with steaming mugs of coffee, Mellie looked at John. He was nibbling on the snacks they'd put out, but his manner was easy. If the Alpha bear was relaxed, things were going well.

Peter sat at Mellie's side, having moved the chair slightly closer to hers than it should be, but she didn't mind too much. She began to sense his bear's need to stake some sort of claim. And judging by the way Paul was looking at her, she was glad of Peter's move.

Paul looked interested. Way too interested. Couldn't he

see she was into Peter? Or was the dragon considering some sort of maneuver around the obstacle that was Peter? That couldn't be allowed. She didn't want the scary dragon. She wanted her Russian teddy bear. Hands down. No contest.

Mellie saw the way Paul looked from her to Peter and back again speculatively, as if he was considering something. Mellie reached over and took possession of Peter's hand, making a clear statement to everyone in the room. No way was she going to let this dragon lothario mess up the best thing that had ever happened to her.

So much for keeping it to herself, but it couldn't be helped. Paul's eyebrow rose impossibly high for a moment, but eventually, he seemed to relax, then nodded and sipped his coffee. Good.

Meanwhile, Peter's bear was rumbling happily at her side. She could feel the vibrations through their joined hands. She didn't dare look at Urse or John. She had a feeling the teasing would begin soon enough, once they were alone.

"I have decided to accept the Alpha's invitation to stay in Grizzly Cove for another day," Paul announced, his accent thick but his English excellent. "I wish to examine the problem you face more closely. I also wish to know more details about the potion you intend to brew and my potential part in it. I would very much like to see the book."

Mellie shot Urse a look, but the grimoire was Mellie's to protect and use for now. "It's not usually done, you understand. This book is ancient and powerful, and it has been entrusted to me for this one specific purpose. I have vowed to protect it, and its many secrets, until my task is complete and then return it to its rightful caretaker."

"You can put a binding on me, if you wish, but I need to see the book before I can make my decision." Paul's voice was firm, and Mellie sensed this was a sticking point for him.

"All right," Mellie conceded, standing. "Give me a moment. I have a binding potion we can use."

Normally, Mellie probably would have asked her sister to take care of it, but this was her task. Her responsibility. And it would be good to show Paul the kind of power she could wield. It would also be a good test for her, as well. Would the dragon be bound by her potion? There was only one way to find out.

Mellie located the small glass bottle she wanted and closed the cabinet door, unsurprised to find that Peter had followed her down the hall and into the room she used to make her potions. She looked at him and put the glass bottle down carefully on the table before moving into his arms.

He hugged her close, rocking her back and forth. His mouth was near her ear, and he kissed her there, gently, before asking. "You okay with all this?"

She sensed he was talking about more than just the presence of the dragon shifter. She had just made a claim on him—albeit a small one, but still a claim—in front of her sister and the Alpha bear. That was something big, and they both knew it.

"I'm okay with you, Peter," she told him honestly, moving back a bit to look into his eyes. "Paul is handsome and incredibly powerful," she admitted, even though Peter's gaze narrowed in annoyance. "But I didn't like the way he was looking at me. I wanted him to know I'm your girl. At least… I want to be your girl, if that's okay." She was laying it on the line, hoping Peter wouldn't let her down.

"Are you kidding?" A smile came over his face that lit her world. "Of course you're my girl. *Zvyozdochka…* I know this is probably the worst time ever to be saying this to you, but I'm really hoping you'll agree to be my mate."

Tears filled her eyes. "Really?" she whispered, overcome with joy and relief. "Oh, Peter!" She reached up and kissed him, happy tears mixing in with the sweetest kiss she had ever known.

When it ended, he kept her close. "Is that a yes?" he asked, and she could see the swirl of magic—the bear spirit—in his eyes. If she accepted him, she would be accepting both of them. The bear and the man. Forevermore.

"It's an emphatic yes," she told him, giving him another

kiss, this time, not mixed with tears, but pulsing with a passion they did not have the time to explore at the moment.

Heavy footsteps were coming down the hall. Dammit. John was coming to check on them. She pulled back from the kiss, spotting her brother-in-law through the open doorway. He was grinning.

"Hey, you two. Did you forget you're entertaining a freaking *dragon* in the kitchen? We're all waiting on you. Hop to it." John's voice was filled with mischievous humor. "There'll be time for that later."

"Go away, John," Peter groused, but he let Mellie go and turned toward the door to usher his Alpha down the hallway. Mellie chuckled as she pulled herself together and followed them.

CHAPTER ELEVEN

"Where's the book?" Paul asked as Mellie returned to the kitchen holding only the potion bottle.

Did he sound just a little too eager? Mellie tried not to worry about showing the book to this relative stranger. The book itself had centuries of protections woven into every page and special magic in the bindings and covers that kept it all much safer than a single witch could hope to do. The book had layer upon layer of witchcraft upon it, but would it be enough to stand up to the dragon's probe, if he had bad intentions?

Mellie certainly hoped so. For now, she had to see if her potions were a match for the dragon shifter's enormous power.

"Here." Mellie slid the potion bottle across the table to Paul. "A standard binding potion. Are you familiar with them?"

"I have come across them a time or two," Paul admitted, taking the small cork out of the top of the bottle and sniffing cautiously.

He used the spoon from his coffee to take a drop of the

liquid out of the bottle and examine its color and consistency. Then, he seemed to focus his gaze on it, and what looked like fire leapt from his eyes to incinerate the droplet of potion in the spoon, sending a puff of clean white smoke upward. Paul nodded then looked back at Mellie.

"It is as you claim," he pronounced. "And very strong. My compliments."

Mellie had never seen anyone do anything like that before. She guessed it was possible that a dragon could shoot fire from his eyes and know a purpose and potency of a magical substance, but it was a new one on her. This day just got stranger and stranger.

"If you'd allow a drop of that to touch your skin and speak the words, I'll allow you to see the book," she told him.

The potion would bind him to whatever promise he made while it was active. So, if he promised not to try to steal the book or use anything he happened to see in it within about five minutes of the potion being absorbed into his skin, then he would be magically bound by that promise forevermore.

Most witches couldn't manage a permanent binding potion, but just like Urse's permanent wards, Mellie's potions were built to last. She would feel much more confident if Paul gave them some promises she could be certain he would keep.

"As you wish," Paul intoned, bowing his head but not breaking eye contact as he held out his left hand and poured a good dollop of the potion into his palm.

He wasn't messing around. Just a drop would have done the trick, and allowing it to be absorbed by his left hand—the one closest to the heart—made the magic even more potent. He had to know that.

"I, Paul Lebchenko, solemnly promise to the good people of Grizzly Cove that I will cause no harm to anyone here who does not first try to harm me. Furthermore, I promise Amelia Ricoletti, the potion *strega*, that I will not try to steal, subvert, or use without permission anything I happen to see in the grimoire that has been entrusted to her care. The book is hers to protect, and I will not attempt anything untoward in the pursuit of my own goals."

Wow. He really was going all out. Mellie felt the binding take hold, and it was a powerful one. As far as she could tell, the dragon's innate magic wasn't repulsing her potion, but blending with it as he took on the binding freely and of his own volition. Voluntary magic was often the strongest kind.

Mellie stood as John thanked the dragon shifter for the promise not to harm anyone in his town. She went back to her spell room and got the book. She couldn't have asked for a more complete statement from Paul. She'd done all she could to be sure his intentions were pure. Now, she would have to trust that her preparations had been thorough enough.

She came into the kitchen, and everyone hushed. The book carried a palpable magic of its own that everyone in the room could feel. She laid the book on the table and held her hands over it. As before, it opened to the page of the spell, and no other.

"This is the potion I propose to brew. Crafted first by *strega* Pilar of Andalusia many generations ago." Mellie noted John craning his neck to try to read the spidery writing on the page along with Paul. Peter had seen it before, as had Urse, so they seemed less interested in the book and more interested in watching the dragon.

"I do not speak this language, but I recognize some words. This is dragon, right?" Paul said, pointing to the word. Mellie nodded. "And that's the word for… Blood?" Paul sounded shocked. Shocked and angry. He rose from his chair rapidly and towered over the table, a hint of his beast showing in his eyes as they grew slitted and inhuman.

Mellie's throat went dry, but she had to fix this. "You're right," she told him in as reasonable a tone as she could manage. "This spell does call for exactly three drops of blood, freely given. It is not, however, the kind of blood magic I believe you are thinking of. It is not evil. Pilar was not evil. She was—if legend can be believed—mated to a dragon. I didn't understand how that could be true until I found out that dragons could be shifters. Pilar was mated to one of your kind, and he allowed her to access his magic in this way. Blood magic of this kind is not evil. It is a benevolent form of self-sacrifice, blessed by the Mother of All."

"I would never allow blood magic in our town," John piped up. "I spoke to the girls' grandmother about this when Urse first told me the details of the spell. I wasn't any more comfortable with the idea of blood used in the ritual than you appear to be," he told Paul. "But I did my research and spoke to Nonna Ricoletti and our shaman, Gus. Since I mated with Urse, I've been learning all sorts of stuff about how humans handle magic that I never knew before." John reached for Urse's hand and shared a loving glance with his wife.

The dragon grew still and watchful, but it could still be seen behind Paul's human eyes. Unearthly. Watching. Measuring. Ready to strike, if necessary.

Scary as hell.

Mellie swallowed hard and tried again. "Shifters mostly know of blood magic because of unscrupulous sorcerers who try to steal other magical folk's power by taking their blood and using it in horrific rites that go against everything we *strega* hold dear." Mellie took a breath, trying to gauge how well her words were being received. "Evil mages will often kill beings of power—other mages, shifters, and Others—to steal their magic. They've even been known to kidnap shifters and hold them captive, bleeding them over a period of time to build up the pain magic and prolong the torture. That is as far from the voluntary giving of three drops of blood under the blessings of the Goddess as you can get. Ask Peter. He participated in my last attempt at this potion, and we actually managed to protect a small part of the beach with that one."

"You did?" Paul's gaze shot to Peter's, skeptical.

"I thought my bear blood might be strong enough to do something, and I would do just about anything for the protection of this place and its people. They are my family, and this place is now my home. There was nothing in the making of the potion that felt wrong," Peter told them all. "Mellie's power is pure and of the Light. I saw it for myself when I agreed to help her with that brew."

Instead of speaking, Paul moved closer to the table, still standing, and held his hand over the open book. He closed his eyes and seemed to reach out with his magic to touch the magic of the book. Mellie could almost see the vast powers intertwining and communicating in some arcane way.

After a moment, Paul dropped his hand to his side and opened his eyes. "The book is neither good nor evil in itself, but the protections laid on it over the centuries are of a benign variety," he pronounced. Again, Mellie was surprised at the things he could discern. Dragons were something special, that was for sure. "I must think about this and seek counsel from the Lady." His eyes looked troubled and still slightly inhuman. "Warn your shaman. I may have need of the standing stones entrusted to his care." Paul turned toward the stairs. "I'll be back in town tomorrow." He shifted his gaze to Peter. "If your grandmother is willing to meet with me, I would still like to talk to her."

"I'll ask her and make the arrangements. I'm pretty sure she'll be intrigued enough to want to meet you," Peter replied.

Paul nodded once, and still looking troubled, he left. Mellie felt her spirits drop.

"Do you think I scared him off?" she asked morosely.

Peter reached out and squeezed her hand, offering comfort. "The blood thing is a tough one," he told her. "We shifters have only known the bad side of blood magic, but I'm confident he'll figure out that has nothing to do with what you propose to do."

"It was brave of you to step up and try to help Mellie," Urse put in, smiling kindly at Peter.

"I could do no less," Peter replied, still holding Mellie's hand.

They sat in an awkward silence for a couple of moments until finally John stood, his chair scraping back loudly against the plank floor. Urse stood a moment later and followed her mate's lead in picking up her empty mug and heading for the sink with it.

The Alpha couple left after just a few more words. Urse made Peter promise to look after Mellie, to which he readily agreed, and John just told them to be careful and to call if they needed backup. Then, they were gone.

"Alone at last," Mellie said, grinning at Peter.

He drew her into his arms and just held her tight for a long moment. So much had happened in such a short time.

"Tell me I wasn't dreaming. You'll be my mate, right?" he whispered, hoping he hadn't misread her response somehow.

"Only if you'll be mine, too," she joked, looking up at him with a light of mischief in her pretty eyes.

"*Zvyozdochka*, I was yours from the moment we first met. It took me a little while to figure it out, but I was a goner even then."

"Really?" Her smile turned coy. "Well, if we're being honest, I'll have to admit that I thought you were hot from the very beginning. I mean, the guys in this town are all pretty amazing, but there was something special about you from the start. I thought maybe it was your accent, but now, I know it's just...you." She ran her hands through his short hair and made him want to revel in her touch. Would she like his bear form as much? He certainly hoped so.

He kissed her. The kiss was filled with the knowledge that they were meant for each other and she had accepted that fact. Satisfaction and yearning for more drove him to lift her up and carry her into her bedroom. There would be no stopping them now. They were mates.

She'd agreed to be his mate. How could a guy get so lucky?

Her clothing joined his on the floor of her bedroom as he worshiped his mate, his love...the one person who was meant for him in all this wide world. Peter made love to her slowly, savoring the experience. It was every bit as powerful as their first time together. Perhaps even more beautiful because, this time, he knew it was the beginning of something that would last a lifetime.

*

Mellie came down slowly from the incredible climax Peter had just given her. They were in her bedroom. Again. He was still inside her as she lay half over him at a somewhat awkward angle. She could fix that…as soon as she caught her breath.

Peter's strong hands roved over her hips and adjusted her. He was so strong. She liked the way he manhandled her as if she weighed no more than a feather. He made her feel feminine in a way she never really had before.

Mellie had always been kind of quirky, with her own sense of oddball style. The men she'd dated in the past had been mere boys compared to Peter. They'd been hipsters and grunge guys. Nerds, for the most part, though there'd been that one metro-sexual dude she'd almost gone for. Peter was a man's man. Like most of the shifter males in Grizzly Cove—according to their mates—he was an animal in bed as well as out of it, and he made her feel like a woman with a capital *W*.

He resettled her more squarely on top of him, still riding his newly hardening cock. The motion renewed her interest, as well, and she started thinking about a long, hard ride. Emphasis on the *hard*.

Peter caressed her breasts as she lifted up, resting on her forearms so she could look into his lovely, intense brown eyes. She could see the bear behind his human gaze at certain moments, and it lit a fire in her veins to know that he was such a powerful being…and that he was all hers.

The possessive feeling was new and thrilling. She'd never been on such secure footing with the man in her bed before. Most of her serious relationships—not that there had been that many—had been less defined. She'd gone into them expecting more, perhaps, but in the end, receiving less than she'd hoped for. None of the men she'd taken into her life had worked out in the end for long-term relationship.

She'd been sad each time she broke up with someone, but quickly realized her heart hadn't been fully engaged in any of those trial situations. She'd been practicing. Waiting for this. For Peter. For the one man designed just for her. The one she would spend the rest of her life loving and living with. Raising children with. Or maybe they'd be called cubs, since some of them would likely inherit their father's shifter nature, though she hoped for at least one little girl of power to carry on the *strega* tradition.

Yeah, she might be getting a little ahead of herself with the daydreams, but it was fun to think about the future with Peter. And it was especially fun to practice the moves that would help populate her future with little mini-me's.

She lifted up higher, sitting hard, taking him deep. Peter was fully erect within her now, his eyes swirling with that dark earth energy that she found so alluring. She could feel their magic sparking off each other, but it wasn't a showy sort of clash. No, they meshed so beautifully that her energy was as low-key as his, though both were pretty intense. Together, they could have created a conflagration, if they both weren't so much in control of their power.

She rode him hard, loving the way her touched her breasts, her body, her hips, guiding her into the motion he wanted on occasion. He let her take the lead for the most part, a willing participant in his own seduction. Mellie felt powerful. Like some sort of femme fatale. Mata Hari at her best. Beguiling and enticing her chosen mark.

Peter grunted as she squeezed his cock from within, using her body to please his in ways she hadn't ever really dared try before. Everything was new with Peter. Her soul was cleansed by his fire. Her heart bathed in his care. She was daring in a way she could never have been with anyone else. Only Peter. Only her mate.

When she came, she screamed his name, triumphant in the

ecstasy they shared. She felt him pulse within her as she froze in a spasm of pleasure so intense it almost blocked out the sun. She felt as if she was part of the Light. Part of the star at the center of existence. Part of the cosmic unity that allowed all beings to have such incredible experiences.

This was what life was all about. Loving and being loved in the most carnal way. Exchanging trust as the most basic level. Being one with another person as pleasure swamped your body and soul.

After that incredible orgasm, Mellie must have dozed because she woke up several hours later, the scent of savory herbs and cooking meat wafting in from her kitchen. Peter must have decided to forage in her fridge for something to eat and discovered the lack of leftovers. She smiled as she tidied herself and pulled on a silky robe she kept at the back of her closet.

They'd missed lunch if the angle of the sun was anything to go by. It looked like it was probably mid-afternoon, but she didn't mind. The bookshop was closed for the day until that uncalled for magic charm dissipated.

Mellie went into the kitchen to find Peter—his muscular chest bare and sexy—just putting the finishing touches on some steaks. Her nose wrinkled as she squinted. There hadn't been any fresh steaks in the fridge.

"I popped down to my shop and restocked your fridge," Peter told her. "You only had rabbit food left, and I'm not big on salad." His grin made her smile in return. The image of a giant bear eating lettuce popped into her head.

She went over to the refrigerator and opened it, surprised to find wrapped cuts of meat of every kind filling most of the previously empty space. He'd put a small fortune in fresh meat in her fridge!

"You didn't need to do that. I meant to go shopping and pick up a few things, but I've been a little preoccupied." She turned back to him. "This is too much, Peter," she told him seriously.

He finished shutting off the burners he'd used and came

over to her. "Nothing is too much for my mate," he said, wrapping his arms around her waist and drawing her close for a deep kiss. Before she completely lost her head, he pulled back. "We should eat before it gets cold."

Ever the gentleman, he escorted her to her seat at the table, pulling out the chair and seeing to her every comfort. He put the plates on the table before taking his own seat. He'd set two places next to each other at some point before she had woken up. He'd thought of everything, it seemed, from the steaks to the wine he served with it, which hadn't been in her apartment that morning.

"Would you come to my den for dinner?" Peter asked her at one point.

"Of course," Mellie replied. "Are you sure your grandmother won't mind? I know she came a long way to see you."

"She will love having you around, believe me," Peter assured her. "I need to talk to her about Paul and see if she will talk with him."

"Do you really think she will?" Mellie asked before taking a bite of her succulent steak, which was cooked to perfection.

"I think so," Peter said, tilting his head as he seemed to ponder the situation. "But my babushka can be contrary sometimes. She isn't always easy to predict."

They talked about his early days, living in Kamchatka and learning from his family and especially his babushka. The meal passed in a haze of happiness, at least on Mellie's part. She couldn't really be sure how Peter was feeling, though he was certainly smiling a lot, so he probably was as happy as she was.

After the excellent steaks were consumed, Peter cleaned up the kitchen while Mellie put the bedroom to rights. She changed the sheets and put the old ones in the washer, along with some other whites that had piled up over the past couple of days. Who had time for housekeeping when you were trying to fight giant, magical sea monsters and entertaining dragons?

When they got to Peter's house late in the afternoon, his grandmother was nowhere to be found. Peter didn't seem worried. Instead, he set to work on dinner preparations after telling Mellie to take a look around the house and get comfortable.

She felt a little strange wandering around his place by herself, so after a cursory look around the living room, which she had seen before in any case, she went into the kitchen area to help him. He didn't say anything about her lack of nosiness, though she thought maybe she'd caught a glimpse of disappointment on his face before he turned away to get something out of the fridge.

He gave her some potatoes to peel and put her to work. They teased each other and stopped for occasional smooches while they worked on the meal. Helping Peter was nothing like cooking with her sister, but it was special in its own way.

"I'm going to have to teach you how to help with some of my Italian specialties," she told him at one point as he seasoned the meat he was working on.

"I love Italian cuisine," he told her. "I guess it's in the blood, seeing as how I just found out the other day that I'm at least part Italian." He grinned at her. "You're going to have to teach me all about my heritage."

"I look forward to it," she told him, meaning it. "Starting with how to make the perfect meatball. What do you say we begin lessons tomorrow?"

"Just tell me what we need, and I'll get it tomorrow," he replied immediately. "I look forward to my first lesson." Then, he paused to kiss her, taking her into his arms and holding her tight.

At some point during the kiss, the front door opened. Peter didn't seem in any hurry to stop kissing her, so she was a little fuzzy on exactly how long the clinch lasted before he released her. Peter had that effect on her. Like a drug to her senses, he could make her lose track of space and time.

All she knew was that when he released her and she opened her eyes to look around, Peter's grandmother was grinning at them from across the room. Blushing, Mellie looked at Peter, but he had a smug smile on his face. She punched him on the arm, but he didn't budge. He merely went back to work on dinner, whistling a jaunty tune.

CHAPTER TWELVE

"It's good to see you two working so nicely together," Granny Ivana said with an undisguised twinkle in her eye.

Peter stopped whistling long enough to greet his grandmother and decline her offer of help with the meal preparations. Granny Ivana took a seat at the kitchen table and supervised instead.

"Did you have a nice walk?" Peter asked his babushka.

"I did. I went down to the beach and saw some of those mer people that live in the water. They seemed very welcoming," she told them.

"They don't just live in the water now," Peter told her. "We're expanding the accommodations in town every day so that more of them can either spend time, or live outright, on land. They've been setting up a branch office of their bank and helping us with some of their extensive business connections. In a few months, you won't even recognize Main Street."

"Is that good or bad?" Mellie wanted to know.

She liked the town the way it was, but she knew there had always been plans to improve the place and invite more industry. The town was just starting out. It couldn't remain as small as it was now, forever.

"Overall, it's a good thing," Peter replied easily. "John has always had big plans. The mer are just helping us realize them sooner, and a lot easier. The whole concept of a bears-only town was novel. Adding mer into the mix was unexpected, but so far it seems to be a blessing."

"There is a good energy about this place," Granny Ivana added, nodding. "The blending of land and sea is unique, but good. It makes both camps stronger."

Peter nodded as he went right on cooking their dinner. "That's exactly what John and the rest of the City Council think. So far, we're ahead of schedule with our plans for the town. By next year, we'll probably have a lot more tourist traffic. Which is why we need to get the magical situation under control as quickly as we can."

"Now, it is probably time for you to tell me about the new presence in your town. The magical currents changed last night, and I sense there is something you wish to tell me," Granny Ivana said ominously.

"Is your grandmother clairvoyant, too?" Mellie asked, almost in awe.

"No. She just knows me better than anyone," Peter admitted with a grin. "Yes, Babushka, there is much I need to say to you. I thought perhaps it would go better over a good meal."

"Trying to soften me up for something?" Granny Ivana asked, her eyes twinkling with mischief.

"Not really," Peter hedged, turning around to look at his grandmother. Mellie stood at the kitchen island, between them. "It's been an eventful day. Mellie, would you do the honors and start the story at the beginning, while I finish up here at the stove?"

Surprised that he'd turned the task over to her, but nonetheless willing, Mellie nodded. As briefly as possible, she told Granny Ivana about the visit from the dragon shifter, Paul, and all that have happened earlier that morning. Granny

Ivana sat silent through the tale, though her eyebrows rose at certain points. Peter helped, adding in details every once in a while from his station at the stove, until Granny Ivana had the basics of the dragon's visit to Mellie's domain.

Granny Ivana sat back and huffed. "Well. You two have had an adventure, it seems."

That was totally not the response Mellie had expected, but it would do. At least the older woman wasn't visibly upset or cursing in Russian.

"Will you meet with him?" Peter asked quietly.

"I think, yes. I should like to see this young dragon. Perhaps he is related to us through my grandfather, or perhaps not, but I would like to see him with my own eyes and get a feel for his energy. Tomorrow, when he comes back to see you, I will be there waiting with you, Mellie," Granny Ivana pronounced, and there was no discussion of the finer points of timing.

If Granny Ivana said something, Mellie got the feeling there was little argument. She could understand why. Granny Ivana had a presence almost as big as the dragon's.

Peter had served up the meal while Mellie had been talking and gathering dishes to set the table. Now, she passed around the plates and silverware as Peter put the finishing touches on the display of mostly meat with a few side dishes. Mellie recognized the potatoes she'd cut up into thin strips earlier. Peter had roasted them in the oven until they were golden brown and seasoned them with herbs. They smelled divine, as did everything he placed in the center of the table.

Once the glasses, plates and utensils had been distributed, and Peter had added a pitcher of iced water with a cut up lemon visible through the glass, they all sat down. Granny Ivana spoke quietly, asking a gentle blessing of the Goddess, and then, they began to eat. Conversation progressed in fits and starts as they consumed what proved to be a delicious meal.

Granny Ivana told them more about her memories of her grandfather, the dragon. She talked of her childhood and the immense power of the grandfather she had loved so much.

"When he left us, it wasn't in the usual way, I recall," Granny Ivana said, her words somewhat distant as if remembering something from the far past. "We didn't have a normal death ceremony for him. I was still quite young and didn't question things, but one day, he just stopped being there. It was as if he'd left on a trip and, then, just never came back," she told them. "I wonder now what really happened to him. I assume he's dead, after all this time, but I assumed that then, and I may very well have been wrong."

"What makes you say that?" Mellie asked, curious.

"Well, he disappeared about a decade or so after his mate died. I remember my grandmother as a very old woman with all the signs of advanced age. She had lived a lot longer than almost any other bear, or so it was said at the time, and she probably would have kept going a bit longer, but there was an accident, and a big tree fell on her. I was a child, but I remember the adults being very upset. Grandpa was inconsolable. I remember my parents being very concerned that he would die soon too, without his mate, but he just got very quiet and distant from us all emotionally, for a long time. He was better with us kids, and I think he stayed as long as he did for us. But, when I was a teenager, he just disappeared and where he'd gone remained a mystery."

"If they were true mates…" Peter offered in a sad voice.

"Yes, I know. It is hard for one of our kind to survive after losing a mate. He could have gone off somewhere to die alone. I'm not really sure what dragons do in such cases." Granny Ivana shook her head, her expression solemn. "None of us were dragons. We didn't share in his gift. We didn't understand him as well as we could have because we didn't understand his animal."

They talked of her recollections of the dragon throughout the rest of the meal. When it came time to start clearing away the dishes, Granny Ivana stood and held up one hand to call for quiet. She then went to the cabinet over the refrigerator that was seldom used and pulled out something in a dish covered tightly with plastic wrap so that not even a hint of a scent could escape.

"Babushka," Peter said with a big grin as his grandmother came closer, unwrapping the plastic as she walked. "You found my secret weapon."

"Secret weapon?" Mellie repeated, curious about the contents of the bowl. Not being a shifter, her nose wasn't as sensitive, and she didn't know yet, without a visual cue, what was in the dish.

"My Peter has been holding out on us," Granny Ivana said with a grin, coming closer to place a huge dish filled with ripe blackberries on the table. "He's got a berry patch on his property that's bigger than any I've ever seen before. Just look at these blackberries!"

"That patch on the side of the hill was one of the main reasons I settled on this particular piece of land," Peter told them proudly. "There's nothing quite like the flavor of blackberries growing wild in the acidic soil of the Pacific Northwest." He reached into the bowl and grabbed a big, juicy berry between his thumb and forefinger and held it up like a connoisseur examining a rare gem.

"Oh, those look delicious," Mellie said when Granny Ivana looked for her opinion. "I love blackberries."

"Good." Granny Ivana took the dish and spooned a big helping onto Mellie's plate without further ado.

There were too many, really. Mellie could only handle a few, but she figured she'd discreetly dump the rest onto Peter's plate at some point in the near future. She knew now that the man could put away food in mass quantities, just like her brother-in-law. These bears knew how to *eat.*

Granny Ivana sat back down after serving them all a big helping of berries, and there was silence for a few minutes while everyone appreciated the fine flavor of the ripe fruit. Peter smiled at Mellie when she pushed a few of her berries onto his plate. Then, he leaned over and gave her a smacking kiss on the lips from which she could taste the flavor of the berries in a way that nearly made her forget they had an audience.

Remembering Granny Ivana's presence, Mellie looked over at the older woman, already blushing as she leaned away from Peter and back toward her own place at the table. Granny Ivana only winked, making Mellie's blush deepen.

Peter cleared his throat and put down his spoon. "Thank you for gathering dessert, Babushka," he told his grandmother formally. "Mellie and I reached an agreement earlier today," he started, taking Mellie's hand in his.

Was he really going to spill the beans like this? Mellie realized his grandmother was probably the first person they should tell about their change in status. She might only be visiting, but she was the elder of the families, in this case, and Mellie figured that would protect her from her sister's wrath at being told later. Mellie had to smile at the idea of Urse's reaction. No doubt, her sister would be happy for them both. Finding your life partner and agreeing to the match was a big deal in both the human and shifter worlds. It was also pretty monumental among *strega*, who tended to walk their paths alone a disproportionate percentage of the time.

"Congratulations," Granny Ivana said even before Peter made the official announcement. "I've been hoping you would find a nice girl for a long time, Peter." Granny Ivana's tone was teasingly scolding. "Now, tell me, are you going to have a human-style wedding?"

Mellie looked blankly at Peter. "We hadn't talked about that at all," she said.

"If that is what you wish, we will do it," Peter told her. "Anything you desire, we will do."

"I haven't told my sister yet," Mellie blurted. "She needs to know before we can start planning anything. And, from what I understand, weddings take a while to plan and work out."

"Then, I suppose I must stay in Grizzly Cove for a while," Granny Invana said with a teasing sigh. "If you have a wedding, I want to be at it."

*

After Babushka had given them both bear hugs and further congratulations, and all the dishes had been put in the washer, Peter took his new mate by the hand and led her outside. He wanted to show her his territory…and his bear. He only hoped she would like his furry side as much as she seemed to like his human half.

"Where are we going?" she asked, tugging on her jacket as they went out the door.

"I want to show you the berry patch," he hedged.

"In the dark?" Her tone was incredulous, but she didn't hesitate to follow where he led. Her trust humbled him, and made him that much more fiercely devoted to her safety.

"I promise, I won't let you get tangled up in the thorns. I just want you to see the extent of my territory… *Our* territory, if you'll consent to come live in my den." They hadn't gotten to the part yet where they discussed living arrangements, but his inner bear was pushing him to get more commitment from her.

She'd agreed to be his mate, but there was more to it than that. The bear wanted to be around her at all times, and all hours of the day and night. The man and bear both wanted to live with her. He'd prefer his den because it was big and comfortable—and most of all, secure. But he'd happily live with her above the bookstore, if that's what she really wanted.

"I suppose we could rent out the apartment," she said in a tentative tone. "I'd have to talk it over with Urse. The place is still half hers. But I know with the mer moving into the cove, available accommodations on land can't quite keep up with the demand. We'd probably be able to get a tenant with no problem at all."

"It's a sound business decision," Peter put in, trying not to crow with victory. "And it would bring in a little extra income for you both."

"I don't think we'd charge a whole lot, but yeah, it could work out really well for everyone," Mellie said. "Urse and I were already discussing hiring someone to help out part-time in the store since she hooked up with John. Understandably, she wants to spend more time with him. If we could find a tenant who wanted to work in the shop with us, they could open, and we both could go in later in the day."

They walked as they talked, the terrain changing only a little as they rose up the side of the hill into which Peter had built his home. He'd picked his spot carefully, choosing an easily defensible place that also had the creature comforts he wanted. His land boasted a small grove of giant sequoia that he was nurturing, as well as the berry patch and a small stream that eventually led down to the cove. On his land, though, the stream had found a small spot in which to pool.

The little watering hole attracted wildlife and was a great spot to picnic in human form. In bear form, it offered a place to cool off in the summer and a year-round place to get a bit of fresh water. His grandmother's scent was all over the place. She'd investigated every inch of his land. He'd love to get her opinion of the place he'd chosen. He suspected she already approved, judging by her reaction to the blackberries.

But Mellie's approval was the most important right now. It certainly sounded as if she would be willing to move to his den, which was a major victory, as far as he was concerned.

If she'd been a shifter, this would have been a lot easier, but with her being human—okay, she was a *strega*, but still basically human with a powerful magical talent—he knew he had to take things more slowly than he would with a shifter mate. He had to finesse her into each step forward. At least, that's what he'd thought, but it was proving easier than he'd expected.

"I'd need a sacred space to do my work," she told him suddenly, returning him to the conversation. "I have the spell room in the apartment, but I could move it here if you give me a spot I can use. Maybe we could dig a little farther into the hill? The constant temperature and lack of sunlight is good for storage of my herbs, but sometimes, I need the sun or starlight to brew by. Maybe we could set up an outdoor area—like a little sacred circle for use as necessary. It doesn't have to be huge, and it can be hidden."

"Would a naturally occurring circle work?" he asked, interested in her needs. He had something in mind, but he wasn't sure what was required.

"Like a stone circle?" she asked. "I know there's one up at the point, but that's kind of far away for casual work, and besides, that's really Gus's place. I wouldn't want to constantly intrude on his territory. I don't need anything that grand."

"What about a circle of trees? Would that work?" he asked.

She paused in her steps and turned to him. "That would be ideal, actually. Healthy trees have positive energy and can sometimes lend their strength to my brews, if they're so inclined. It depends what type of tree, though. Something with a straight, nearly bare trunk makes the best circle, but I can work within a variety of species."

"Do you see the towering giants over there?" Peter paused and pointed to their left. The stars gave him plenty of light to see by, but he supposed the trees were just distant shadows to Mellie. Her next words confirmed it.

"I can't see in the dark like you, Peter," she admitted quietly, as if it were something shameful.

He put his arms around her and held her close. "Never feel bad about being exactly who and what you are. I'm sorry. I didn't mean to imply anything negative. It was just a question. No judgment. I promise."

She peeled back from him to look into his eyes. "I can see you, but mostly what I see of you is your magic. It almost lights you from within in this setting," she admitted.

"I love the way you see me, *zvyozdochka*," he whispered, before lowering his lips to hers.

The kiss was magic. The night breeze blew around them, encasing them in the stillness of the dark. The breathless hush of the forest.

An owl hooted, and Peter remembered why he'd brought

her out here. He had two things to show her. Leaning away, he broke the kiss and took her hand in his as he let her out of his embrace. She seemed hesitant to leave his arms, which made him feel ten feet tall.

"Come. I have things to show you." Holding her hand, he led her around the side of the hill behind the house.

They came out into a clear spot that was roughly above the inner rooms he had excavated behind the natural cave around which he'd built his home. There were no giant trees up here, only brambles and a huge berry thicket. The blackberries were ripe now, but at other times of the year, other berry varieties made their presence known up here in smaller quantities.

"Do you smell the berries?" he asked, breathing deep. The scent of ripe blueberries was nearly overwhelming to his senses, so even her duller nose would probably pick up something.

"I do. Is this where Granny Ivana got the blackberries?" she asked, moving a few steps into the pathway he'd begun to cultivate.

"It is. And there are other things growing up here, too. I thought maybe we could set aside some spots up here for any herbs you might want to cultivate. We could do natural-looking scatter plantings so nobody would realize this is your garden, since it's the one spot on my property that's this exposed from the air. Would that work for you?"

She turned to him, her eyes sparkling with joy in the starlight. "I would love that!" She put her arms around him this time, giving him her best approximation of a bear hug. "Are you sure you wouldn't mind?"

"Mind? *Zvyozdochka*, everything I do, from now on, I do for you. For us. I don't mind one bit."

Her breath caught at his words and she buried her head against his neck, hugging him close. "You're an amazing man, Peter."

"Ah, but that's just it. I'm not just a man, Mellie. I want you to meet my bear. I want to know if you can accept the other side of me."

"Here? Now?" Mellie's first thought was that Peter had to be nuts. He'd picked a dark forest as the scene to introduce his scary bear form to her? What was he thinking?

Then again, it was Peter. He would never hurt her. She knew that down to the depths of her soul. It didn't matter where they were or if the sun was shining or not. No matter what, he would never harm her.

"If you'd rather wait, I can, but this is something that's been on my mind. Frankly, my bear is worried that you won't like us in that shape."

For the first time, she heard doubt in Peter's voice. Her big, strong bear-man was worried. Damn. She couldn't let that continue. It was in her power to end his anxiety and she damned well better do it.

"Let's not wait. Go furry for me, Peter. I promise I won't be scared."

Okay, maybe she was stretching the truth a little bit. She wasn't exactly sure if she could control the basic human instinct to be a little apprehensive when faced with a large predator with very sharp claws. But it was *Peter*. She had to keep reminding herself of that. She would do anything for him, and she was beginning to believe that he would do the same for her.

"All right," Peter said, his hands already tugging off his clothing. "Here's the plan. I'm going to shift. Then, I'll just stand over here and give you a chance to get used to me in my other form. If you're okay with that, then we can walk over to another spot I want to show you. If you wouldn't mind bringing my clothes along, I'd appreciate it." His rueful smile made her chuckle.

"So, that's why you wanted me to come walking with you. I'm the pack mule."

"Never that, *zvyozdochka*. I brought you out here because I wanted to spend time with you and show you my territory. The fact that you can carry stuff for me while I go bear is just a bonus." He leaned in to give her a smacking kiss as he handed her the neat pile of his clothes. "Now, watch. I will go straight to my full bear, but you will see the battle form in the middle of the change where I'm about half and half. I only stay in that form when it's truly necessary," he told her.

Mellie knew from talking to Urse that the battle form was the most deadly. But it was also the hardest to maintain, and most shifters couldn't manage to hold it for any length of time at all. The fact that Peter could, told her a lot about the strength of the man, and the bear. In any other animal species, he would have been an Alpha leading dozens of other shifters, but bears were a little different. They mostly roamed alone and this group had chosen John to be the Alpha because he was the best strategist of their old unit.

Several of the other guys—including Peter—could easily have been Alpha, but they'd all agreed to follow John's vision. They weren't blindly obedient, hence the town council that made a lot of significant decisions, but they were behind John's vision pretty much one hundred percent.

As Mellie watched, Peter called upon his magic, and the shift began. He was surrounded by a nebulous cloud of his magic that she could see against the dark of the night. He went from big man to even bigger half-man-half-bear, and then, he dropped down onto all fours, fully bear. Enormous bear. Giant freaking scary bear.

Mellie did her best to regain her calm. Her breathing had sped up, and a bit of adrenaline had hit her system in the classic fight-or-flight response, but she knew in her heart that this was Peter. He wouldn't hurt her.

As he remained still, simply standing about four feet away from her, she remembered what he had told her of his plan for how this encounter would go. So far, he was sticking to the plan, which was very reassuring.

Hesitantly, Mellie made herself take a step forward. This was Peter. She needed to be comfortable with every manifestation of him. Her heart wouldn't allow her to hurt him in any way, and if she was afraid of his bear form, she knew he would be hurt.

He stayed still while she edged closer. Maybe talking to him would help.

"Peter? You're kind of freaking huge, you know?" The bear made a snuffling sound that resembled quiet laughter. "Can I touch your fur?" she asked before reaching out. Maybe, if she felt the warm fur under her hands, she might calm a little more.

The bear raised and lowered his head in a nod. Mellie moved closer. He hadn't made a single threatening move yet, and she was beginning to come to terms with the massive predator that was her boyfriend. She giggled as she touched her hand to his auburn fur. She could see little sparks of magic at the contact in the starlight.

"Man, you're soft." When he moved into her touch, her fingers sank deeper into the fluffy fur behind his ear. She was standing at his side, away from the very sharp teeth that gleamed in the darkness. "Your magic is much closer to the surface in this form, isn't it?" she asked rhetorically. She could feel it buzzing against her fingers, a lovely tingle that made her feel truly alive.

It calmed her even more until all trace of the adrenaline rush was gone. It might come back if he did something scary, but for now, she was getting more comfortable with him in this form. She held his clothes over one arm and kept her other hand on his shoulder.

"So, what did you want to show me next?"

With an approving little growl, he began to walk, and she stayed at his side as they moved through the forest, away from the open spot where the berries grew and back into the trees. She kept in contact with him at all times, and she knew he was probably walking really slow to accommodate her much shorter legs and stride size.

Before long, though, they came to an area where the tree trunks were absolutely huge. Entranced by the feeling of the place, Mellie let her hand drift away from Peter's side as she moved closer to the dark sentinels she sensed rather than actually saw in the darkness.

"Are these giant sequoia?" She knew her whispered words were filled with the awe she was feeling. The giant trees were some of the most ancient and magical life forms left on the planet. "Sweet Mother of All," she whispered as she moved into the space between two massive trunks. She felt the bear following her, watching intently.

There were four giant trees altogether. Spaced far enough apart that they each had room to grow, but the impossible thing was that—if she wasn't very much mistaken—they were at the four cardinal points. One was due North. One was South. One East and one West. Impossible.

If it were almost any other tree, Mellie would assume someone had planted them in these specific spots, but these trees had to be ancient. She had no idea if there had even been people in this region at the time these forest giants began their lives in this spot.

"Magic?" she wondered aloud. Had someone or something caused this incredible space to be formed at the center of these giants? "Or the hand of the Goddess?" That seemed more likely to her at the moment, considering the recent appearance of a sacred circle of stones on the southern point of the cove, not for from here.

"Maybe this spot was designed just for you." Peter's voice came from behind, and she spun to face him.

He came to her, in the exact center of the clearing, and put his arms around her. He was naked. Warm. Still sparking magic from what must have been a quick shift from bear to human form.

"Look up," he whispered.

She did as he instructed, and gasped. The towering trees formed a perfect circle with their branches high above. She could clearly see the stars, far, far away.

"This is amazing," she whispered, reverent in this natural cathedral.

"It's a sacred space," he agreed. "One in our territory, just waiting for you, my mate. Think of all the good you can do with rituals and potions you brew here."

She looked back down to Earth, catching Peter's eye. He understood. She saw it in his gaze, in his caring expression.

"You get me," she told him, emotion welling up in her chest. "All I've ever wanted to do with my magic was help people. It's my *raison d'etre*, or so Nonna has always says. I'd like to set up here and do things in the sacred circle of these trees to help everyone in Grizzly Cove. Maybe even people beyond. With a place like this, I think I could do a lot of good."

The wind picked up, and a sparkling song filtered through the branches of the giant sequoia. It almost sounded like approval.

CHAPTER THIRTEEN

It was really late by the time they returned to the house. They'd both sort of lost track of time in that sacred space, just holding each other quietly and listening to the wind. It had felt like a benediction. A welcoming. An inevitable twist of fate that had brought them together with that incredible place.

"Will you stay with me tonight?" Peter asked her in a low, sexy tone that made her knees weak.

"What about your grandmother?" Mellie's human sensibilities wouldn't change overnight.

Peter came to her as she stood by the banked fire in the fireplace. "In the eyes of my people, we are mates. We're already married, to use the human word. We should not be apart. Babushka will not bat an eye that we sleep together, only if we sleep apart. She knows how hard it is for newly mated shifters to be parted from their mate."

"You'll suffer if I say I want to leave?" she asked, already having made up her mind that she would stay, but she was interested. She wanted to know all the rules of his world.

"I would just follow you home and stay in the apartment

with you again," he said philosophically. "Of course, if you kicked me out, I would go, but I would probably shift and sleep in the woods behind your store all night, keeping watch."

"That is so sweet. Sad, and a little scary, but sweet." She brushed his hair back from his forehead and smiled at him. He was such a good man. "I'll stay. Of course, I'll stay. But, first thing tomorrow, we have to tell Urse and John, okay? She's going to be mad enough at me as it is for not telling her right away."

"Deal," he told her, swooping down to lift her into his arms.

He walked her into the back of the house, taking her to a door that was standing ajar. What she could see of the room beyond looked masculine and large. Was this the master bedroom? She certainly hoped so.

The walls were painted a rich cream color, and wood accents abounded from the crown molding to what looked like a handmade four poster bed, complete with curtains in a rich brocade fabric. It was manly, yet opulent, at the same time. Peter's Russian heritage showing through, no doubt.

Gold and burgundy seemed to be the theme, along with golden wood and cream on both the walls and bedding. It was gorgeous. Sumptuous and inviting.

"Do you like it? We can change the décor to anything you want," Peter said as he laid her down on the huge bed.

"It's beautiful," she said simply, reaching up to cup his cheek. "I think I could be very happy here."

The smile that lit his face shone in his eyes, as well. He drew closer, kissing her with all the joy she'd seen in his expression. She was home. She'd never felt quite the same before and doubted she ever would again. Only with Peter. Wherever they were—if they were together—she was at home.

As he kissed her, he undressed her. She was glad he'd taken the initiative because she wanted to feel his skin against hers as soon as possible. She got her wish as their breathing intensified and the passion rose between them. Soon, there was no fabric impeding her desire to touch him all over.

She had reveled in the feel of his skin back in the circle of towering giant trees, but the moment had been a quiet one, not meant for fiery passion. No, that moment had been filled with amazement at the place and the man and the beast he had become, who had walked at her side calmly through the midnight woods. The predator had been her protector, and she'd come to learn that he would forever be at her side, never a threat to her—only to those who might seek to harm her.

That moment had been a benediction of their relationship, witnessed by the ancient power of the towering trees. It had lasted a long time. A simple embrace in the dark under a canopy of starlight let in through the perfect circle formed by the upper branches of the giant sequoia.

This, though… This was different. This was a time just for the two of them. Man and woman. Lovers eternal.

There were no witnesses, silent trees or sparkling stars. Not this time, though she couldn't rule out the possibility in the future. This was just Peter and Mellie, together, teaching each other the ways of their love.

Her heart was bursting with the emotion, though they hadn't really spoken of it yet. She suspected he loved her but just hadn't gotten around to saying it. Maybe he was waiting for her? Maybe he needed a little nudge?

Either way, she wouldn't let him go on assuming they'd spend the rest of their lives together until he came out and told her he loved her. Mellie needed to hear it. She knew herself well, and not hearing those words would drive her around the bend in the end. Better to end the uncertainty now, early in the game.

Daring greatly, she pushed back from his drugging kiss and looked into his confused eyes. She knew he was going to ask what was wrong, but she preempted him.

"Do you love me?" she asked in rush.

"What?" He seemed shocked by her question.

"Do you love me?" she repeated, holding her breath as she waited for his answer.

"Of course, I love you, *zvyozdochka.* You are my mate." He said it as if it should go without saying, but she'd needed to hear the words. Her heart filled with joy and probably showed on her face.

"For the record, I love you, too, Peter. I just needed to hear it," she told him.

"Then, I will tell you of my love as often as you like," he told her very seriously. "I will give you whatever you need. As your mate, my number one priority now is your happiness and wellbeing." He kissed her between words of that last sentence. Little nibbling kisses all over her face and neck, reigniting the flame of desire within her. "I love you," he whispered as his lips went lower. "I love you," he said again as his mouth hovered over her breast, his hot breath tormenting her sensitive skin in the most delicious way.

He lowered his mouth, taking the tip into his mouth and laving the engorged skin in ways that made her whimper and writhe. He knew just how to touch her to make her his. He repeated his words of love as he worked his way over her body, kissing and licking, leaving her in no doubt whatsoever that he really did love her and didn't mind saying the words.

After tonight, Mellie knew she would never be the same. And, when he joined their bodies together, she was the one screaming about love as he began to move with wild abandon. This lovemaking was like no other they had shared before.

He paused at one point, after a small climax, to let her catch her breath and change positions, and she had to ask, "Are the walls soundproofed?"

She hoped they were and had the feeling they might be, but she needed to know after the ruckus they were making. His grandmother was in the house somewhere. It would be really embarrassing if they kept the older woman awake with their shenanigans.

"Each room in the back of the house is dug into a separate

area of the hill. Babushka's room is at the far end from us, so there's plenty of solid earth between us. Plus, I think she probably went out for the evening. She likes to roam in her bear form, in the darkness when nobody can see her."

"Thank the Goddess," Mellie whispered, catching her breath.

Peter chuckled before he started moving again, stealing her breath once more as their passion rose even higher than before. She cried out his name over and over as she came, almost sobbing with the intensity of the orgasms he gave her, until he finally joined her in bliss.

They slept in each other's arms and woke only to make love again in the pre-dawn light.

*

The next morning, the very first thing on Mellie's agenda was to talk to Urse, but her plans got changed when the dragon-man showed up on her doorstep. Peter had come with Mellie to the bookshop early then had gone down the street to the bakery to get breakfast for them both. He had to open his shop later, but they'd planned to have breakfast together before opening their respective shops.

Mellie planned to talk to Urse when she arrived at the shop. She knew her sister's schedule by now. Urse would want to spend the early morning with John before he went to work as mayor. Then, she would make her way to the shop and spend the next few hours with Mellie. That was the perfect time, Mellie thought, to break the news.

But the dragon had other ideas.

Paul showed up at the bookstore while Peter was at the bakery, throwing Mellie's carefully devised plans into chaos. She let him in, having already established with Peter when they'd arrived that the charm the dragon had used on the premises the day before had dissipated.

"Paul. What brings you here so early?" she greeted him at the door. She was reluctant to let him into the shop without anyone else around. She'd already run afoul of his casual use of magic once before, and she didn't really know him well enough to be comfortable in his presence.

"I need to speak with you," he said, his tone a bit on the urgent side. He didn't look like he'd slept at all. In fact, he looked as if he'd been involved in a fight of some kind, when she took a hard look at him.

She still wasn't sure about letting him in, but then, she spotted Peter coming down the sidewalk with John and Urse at his side. They were talking intensely and walking fast. Mellie opened the door, letting Paul in while she waited for the rest of them to arrive.

She didn't have long to wait. Peter had his hands full with bags from the bakery, but he stopped to drop a quick kiss on Mellie's lips as she held the door for him. John and Urse were right behind him, Urse giving her sister a scowling look as she passed into the bookshop.

"I'm glad you're all here," Paul started talking even before Mellie closed the door behind her sister. "I investigated your claims last night and have reached some conclusions."

Paul's accent grew thicker when he was agitated, as he was now, Mellie observed. Peter's did the same thing, but it took a lot to agitate a bear. Paul was probably the same. Whatever he'd learned last night had him in the dragon shifter equivalent of a tizzy. Mellie grew very concerned.

"Gus told me you used the stone circle," John put in, moving some chairs around to form a small circle where they could all sit and talk.

The sisters kept a few small tables and chairs in the store so people could sit and peruse the books before buying. They also came in handy in situations like this, when the bookshop had visitors who wanted to sit and talk.

"I performed a Goddess rite in the circle last evening, and the leviathan went crazy. The Mother of All granted me the vision of what I must do, and though I'm still skeptical, She hasn't steered me wrong yet. I will give you the drops of blood you require, but I want to be present to oversee their use. My blood is more powerful than you know, and I don't give it away lightly," he told Mellie, a stern note in his voice.

She nodded. "That's very understandable, and no problem at all. Peter was present when I used his blood for the potion. I don't mind a small audience, and your active participation will help the potion be even stronger."

"I studied your leviathan and its followers as closely as I could last night," Paul went on. "I even tested the waters, diving down into them well beyond the strong ward around your cove. I was immediately set upon by the creatures in the area and barely escaped back to the air before the big one came. That is no creature to mess around with." Paul looked suitably concerned. "Even the small ones are very dangerous. I almost didn't get away," he confessed, looking really pissed about that particular point. "I have felt its evil now, and you will have my full support in your plan to drive the creatures away from shore."

"Thank you," Mellie said quietly, knowing what a big deal it was that he'd agreed to help.

"Eventually, of course, this creature and its followers must be banished back to where they came from, but for now, protecting the innocent lives on the shore is a good mid-term goal," Paul allowed.

"It's the task I was given," Mellie told him, feeling a bit put out that he seemed to be marginalizing her contribution when it had been so hard for her to get even this far.

Peter put his arm around her shoulders, offering silent support. He understood her moods now, and their closeness would only grow deeper over time. She couldn't wait.

"Is there something you two forgot to tell us?" Urse asked, cutting through Mellie's happy feelings.

Shit.

"Um… I'd planned to tell you this morning, sis, but things just sort of happened…" Mellie gestured to the group gathered around.

"Mellie and I are mates," Peter pronounced in that stoic Russian way of his. Mellie was a little appalled but, at the same time, glad it was finally out in the open.

For a beat, there was no reaction, then Urse jumped up out of her chair and ran around to hug Mellie first, then Peter. John added his congratulations as he shook Peter's hand, and even Paul was quick to congratulate them. Urse had tears in her eyes, and Mellie took her aside for a few private words in the back room.

"I'm so happy for you, Mel," Urse said as they sought a few moments alone.

"I'm just sorry I didn't tell you sooner. Something always got in the way," Mellie said.

"How long have you known?"

"It became official last night, but Peter's grandmother found out first. Sorry," Mellie admitted.

Urse waved the apology away. "I don't care, as long as you're happy. Does Peter make you happy, Mel?"

"Happier than I can put into words," she said on a soft note.

Urse sighed, a silly grin on her face. "Yeah. I know exactly what you mean. Those bear shifters really know how to treat a gal. And my John is the best."

"No better than my Peter," Mellie said, laughing as she put her arm around her sister's shoulders. "How did we get so lucky?"

Urse looked out at the men still sitting in the shop area and tensed. "Hey! They're eating all the pastries!"

CHAPTER FOURTEEN

Mellie spent the rest of the day making preparations for the potion she would brew, with Paul's help, later that night. Paul had gone to the clinic to see Sven, the town's doctor, after their meeting broke up. John had escorted him personally. It turned out that Paul had some serious injuries hiding under his clothing. His brush with the leviathan and its minions had been even worse than he'd described.

The good news was that he would recover fully, given a little bit of time. His dragon constitution would have him back to fighting form in time for the potion brewing that night—or so he claimed. Peter had spoken to Sven personally and had a good idea now of what dragon magic could heal.

Peter took only a few hours away from the bookshop to go over to his own shop. He'd set up an appointment with a mer fellow who had some experience as a butcher. It turned out that mer really liked to diversify away from fish when they were on land, and the man had an impressive resume for a dude who spent a lot of time out at sea.

They went over the setup in the shop, and Giles—that was the mer guy's name—was happy to demonstrate some of his carving skills, as well as discuss his knowledge of the specialty meats Peter stocked for the delectation of the rest of the people in town. At one point, the Cajun black bear, Zak Flambeau, came over to talk about a special order for his restaurant, and Giles was able to provide a new contact down south for the gator meat Zak was after.

They came to terms, and Peter hired Giles to help out at the shop. The business was getting enough traffic that Peter needed the help, and now, with the extra income from supplying Zak's restaurant, he could easily afford it. Thank goodness.

Peter left Giles with Zak. The two men were comparing notes about Cajun meats and suppliers, and Zak had spent enough time in Peter's shop that he could easily show Giles how to close up. Zak knew—as did all of the inner circle—what Mellie had been trying to do. Even if news of their mating hadn't yet spread, Zak didn't mind helping out so that Peter could get back to the bookstore.

Zak was still a deputy sheriff, though Peter had been added to the staff so Zak could have nights free to start his restaurant. At some point, Zak was probably going to stop working for the sheriff and do the restaurant thing full-time. Most likely, that would happen when the restaurant was running at full capacity and tourists were actually coming through town on a more regular basis.

Zak probably knew about the dragon in town from Brody, the sheriff, who had likely been briefed by John. They were all former comrades-in-arms and part of the inner circle that made up the town council. No doubt, news of Peter's mating with Mellie would now pass from John to the rest of the guys, along with the fact that Mellie was about to attempt a very big magical potion.

The guys knew enough not to intrude on that delicate work, but Peter suspected that after the potion was done, there would be a party. Bears liked to celebrate, and a mating was always a great reason to throw a bash. He didn't think Mellie would mind. In fact, it would likely impress upon her that not only had she joined her life to Peter's, but now she would forever be part of the larger community of shifters in Grizzly Cove.

When Peter got back to the bookshop, Urse was manning the store, and she told him that Mellie was still upstairs in the apartment, holed up in her potion room. Lunch had come and gone, and dinner wasn't too far away. Peter went up to the apartment and began cooking. He'd restocked Mellie's fridge with meats from his shop, and it was a simple matter to get something started for them to eat when she emerged from her work.

Paul was still down at the clinic, catching up on some healing sleep under Sven's watchful eye. They'd prearranged to have the dragon shifter arrive just before moonrise, when the real work on the potion would begin, according to Mellie. Peter would be on hand throughout, ready to help his mate in any way she needed.

The rest of his old Army unit would also be on high alert tonight and were quietly preparing to back Peter up when he and Mellie headed to the point near the stone circle where she would release her potion into the water. Peter figured it couldn't hurt to have a few more guys around, helping keep things secure. Especially if the leviathan decided to object, which Peter assumed was going to happen regardless what they did.

Mellie came down the hallway just as the food was finishing cooking. She was rubbing the back of her neck and looked a bit worn down. No doubt, she'd been expending energy—both magical and mundane—preparing for the final steps of the potion she would brew tonight.

"Thank you for cooking," she said as she walked up to Peter and gave him a gentle kiss on the cheek. "I'm sorry you've had to do so much of it just lately, and I promise this isn't how it will always be. I love to cook, and I'll dazzle you with my Italian cuisine one of these days."

"I have no doubt about that, *zvyozdochka*. But you are busy just now with the potion, and this is the least I can do. I don't expect my mate to wait on me hand and foot. We are a team now. A partnership." He ushered her to the table where he'd already set places and was just now placing the final serving platter.

"I like the sound of that," she told him, smiling as she sat down. "This looks wonderful."

They didn't speak much after that, enjoying the meal in relative silence as they chewed and swallowed. Weighty thoughts were on both of their minds. Peter worried for his new mate and the task she would attempt to complete tonight. He supposed she was contemplating the spell she would cast. He suspected they were both concerned about the dragon shifter's participation.

Although Paul seemed like a reasonable fellow, he was still a bit of an unknown quantity. And his magic was wild in comparison to Peter's. Bears were strong in their magic, but this dragon was off the charts. Even though Peter had dragon blood far back in his ancestry, and was therefore a little more powerful than most bears, Paul was something completely out of Peter's experience.

Only Babushka, of all the people in Grizzly Cove, had any experience whatsoever with a dragon shifter, and that had been when she was a little girl. Hundreds of years ago. And the dragon in question had been a relative, someone who cared for her and her safety. Paul had no such ties to this community. While he spoke well and said all the right things, until he actually did something to prove his worth, Peter would remain on guard. It was only the sensible thing to do.

They finished the meal, and Peter shooed Mellie to the couch. "You have about an hour before moonrise. Relax and close your eyes for a bit. Rest up for what comes later," Peter advised her.

Mellie didn't argue. She went to the big overstuffed sofa and put her feet up. Peter worked as quietly as he could, cleaning up in the kitchen. The open concept floorplan of the apartment meant he could keep watch over her while she rested.

Forty minutes later, Peter heard the arrival of the dragon shifter as he talked quietly with Urse in the shop below. Urse sent Paul to the back stairs while she greeted her mate, John, and locked the front door to the shop, then she followed Paul toward the back stairs with John in tow. Peter could hear all of this in the quiet of the apartment, his shifter hearing giving him the audible cues that Mellie totally missed.

He went to her and woke her with a kiss. Drawing away, he smiled at her. "Paul, Urse and John are on their way up."

Mellie stretched as she sat up while Peter went to open the door for the new arrivals. He exchanged greetings with them all as they entered, and soon, all five were standing in the main area of the apartment. Mellie was nervous, but that was understandable. Still, she took charge when it was clear nobody else was going to speak first.

"Paul and Peter, if you'll come with me into the potion room, we can get started on this. John and Urse, if you wouldn't mind observing from out here?" Mellie asked politely. The Alpha couple agreed with nods, and Urse whispered a quick *good luck* to her sister as Mellie turned to lead the way down the hall toward the room set aside for crafting her potions.

Peter let Paul precede him down the hallway, keeping an eye on Mellie as she opened the door. Paul went in after her, and Peter brought up the rear. The small room was crowded with all three of them in there, but it would do.

As before, when Peter had been the one giving blood to the spell, Mellie explained what she would do, and Paul moved into position. At the appointed time, Mellie began her chant, and Paul used his own fingernail—partially shifted into a sharp talon—to prick a finger on his left hand. When the first drop of his blood hit the potion, there was an audible rumble, and the building shook slightly.

Mellie's eyes widened, and Peter scowled. He could feel the intensity of the magic. *This* was what had been lacking the last time she'd brewed this potion. This—if it kept growing, as Peter suspected it would—would be a potion to reckon with even the leviathan.

"Um…I think maybe we ought to do the rest of this outside. And away from the center of town," Mellie said in a hesitant whisper, as if merely speaking too loud might set the earth to rattling again. "Peter, could you drive us down to the point? Once we hit the final stage with this, it'll probably be way too potent to contain. We'll have to unleash it right away."

"Sounds like a good plan," Peter replied immediately, grinning at her, even as he thought through the logistics. "Paul, do you mind relocating this to where it can do the most good?"

"Not at all," Paul answered politely, his eyes narrowed. "I take it you didn't expect this?"

Mellie was carefully bottling her potion and preparing to take it on the road, but she spared a glance and a smile for Paul. "I've done this potion before, but without the missing ingredient, it didn't have nearly this kind of whammy. Now, I understand why the recipe is kept only in the grimoire. If an unethical mage had this knowledge, and access to the blood of one of your kind, this potion could do a lot of damage. As it is, I hope it will do a lot of good to protect the people along this coast."

"You still propose to try and cover the entire coast? Not just your town?" Paul asked.

"I want to protect as many innocents as possible from the leviathan and its minions. If this potion will protect many, then it would be selfish and wrong to keep it for just a few," Mellie told him.

Paul smiled. "I may have misjudged you, *Strega* Ricoletti. Forgive me."

Mellie nodded, and the three of them headed out of the room. Mellie asked Urse to grab a few things on the way out, and Peter noted that her sister didn't ask questions but started packing a tote bag while Mellie ever-so-carefully made her way down the stairs, keeping both eyes on the extraordinary potion in her hands.

Peter escorted her and her precious cargo to his vehicle and helped her get in. He let Paul fend for himself, focusing on Mellie and barely noticing Paul as he climbed into the backseat. When everyone was secure and the potion was as protected as they could make it, held tight in Mellie's careful hands, Peter pulled out onto the road, driving slowly and steadily toward the point. Thankfully, the road was still too new to have any potholes, but Peter was extra careful, just in case.

John and Urse followed along in the mayor's SUV as they all made their way toward the point. The rest of the team was already spread out around the point, and the guys who had been stationed in town were following, Peter was confident. They took care of their own.

Going off-road was a bit of a challenge when they came to the turnoff that would take them to the circle of stones. They didn't dare put in a road or even mark a path to the sacred site. This place was not for tourists, and the less humans knew about its existence, the better.

Nevertheless, Peter knew exactly where to head, though he did so at a snail's pace so as not to shake up Mellie's potion too badly. Who knew what would happen if that brew got overly excited?

Mellie's eyes were on the potion bottle in her hands whenever Peter glanced at her. He didn't blame her. He'd felt the earth tremble at the first drop of the dragon's blood.

"That's some potent shit you've got in your veins, Paul," Peter rumbled as they inched toward the stone circle.

Paul chuckled. "I've never known anything else. I was born this way."

"My grandmother said she tried to visit you in the clinic this afternoon, but you were asleep," Peter told the dragon shifter.

"I'm sorry to have caused her a wasted trip," Paul said politely. "I was unprepared for my encounter with the leviathan earlier, but I've got its number this time."

"It cannot be killed in this realm," Peter warned him. "All

our experts agree that it can only be banished back to where it came from or trapped in another realm. It can't be killed, so don't waste your time trying."

"Maybe I can't kill it, but I can certainly teach it a lesson," Paul growled, his expression darkening as light flickered behind his eyes.

Peter saw it all in the rearview mirror and marveled at the way the dragon's growl sounded totally different than a bear's growl. They might both be shifters, but they were worlds apart as far as their beasts went.

"If this works the way I hope it will, *I'll* be the one teaching it a lesson," Mellie piped up, easing the tension in the air. "With your help, of course."

Paul nodded in acknowledgment of her claim and subsided.

"There are others here," Paul said a moment later as they neared the site. He was scanning the terrain out the window.

"It's my team," Peter told him. "You didn't think the guys would let us do this alone, did you?" He addressed his words to Mellie, though Paul heard him, too. "We're a unit, and you're part of it now, Mellie. You're my mate, which means every one of my brothers-in-arms will protect you in my place, if necessary. You're one of ours now."

"Really?" Mellie's voice held a hint of awe, and she looked into Peter's eyes as he drew the truck to a stop just outside the stone circle. Her eyes held traces of wonder, even as they sparkled with unshed tears.

Peter reached out, putting one hand over hers. "Really, *zvyozdochka*. Now and forevermore."

The moment was broken by the click of the back door opening as Paul let himself out. Peter sighed, but Mellie squeezed his hand.

"Don't think badly of him," Mellie whispered. "I know, from watching Urse with John, it's kind of hard to witness someone else's happiness when you're alone."

"You have a kind heart, my love. And neither one of us will ever be alone again. Not if I have anything to say about it," he reassured her, leaning in to place a quick kiss on her lips.

He let himself out then came around to help her down. She was carrying that slightly dangerous potion, and he wanted to make sure there were no mishaps on the way into the stone circle. Gus was waiting for them, already speaking in low tones with Paul.

Unlike the rest of the team, Gus wasn't armed with conventional weapons. He would go bear if he needed to help defend the happenings in the circle against outside interference.

"Hi, Mel," Gus greeted Mellie casually, as if she wasn't holding a half-finished potion that had caused the earth to move.

"Hey, Gus." Mellie was just as casual with the town's shaman, though they weren't really that close. "I'm sorry to barge in, but you felt that a few minutes ago, right?" She had a slightly embarrassed smile on her face.

Gus smiled back kindly. "It was hard to miss. But we shouldn't have any more trouble if you confine the magic to the circle until it's ready to be unleashed."

"Yeah, I probably should've done that in the first place, but up to this point, the potion has never been that…um…violent when I brewed it before," she explained.

Gus chuckled. "Well, you never had the right ingredients before either."

"Good point," she agreed easily. "Let me just set this up on the altar and get everything consecrated," she said, heading into the circle of stones.

Peter and Paul stood on either side of Gus, just outside the circle, watching Mellie set up. Peter was aware of the rest of his unit forming up in a loose circle around them. Most of the guys were armed with the biggest, baddest firepower they could beg, borrow or steal. All bets were off going up against the leviathan and its minions. There was even a Jeep rigged with a fifty-caliber machine gun, like something straight out of the desert combat units they had once fought alongside.

Paul noticed, too, his eyebrows rising. "Your people seem loaded for bear," he observed.

Gus laughed aloud, and Peter growled. "That's a term we don't really like," Peter told the dragon shifter.

Paul looked surprised, realization dawning. "My apologies. No offense intended. It's just a saying, you know?"

"We know!" chorused all the bear shifters within hearing, causing Gus to laugh even harder. He, of all the bears from the old unit, seemed to find the oddest things funny. Probably went with being a shaman and spooky-assed spirit bear.

Paul looked around, nodding apologetically and sharing smiles with some of the other guys. "I've learned my lesson. I will try not to ever use that expression again."

This time, the chorus said, "Thank you," in unison, in a somewhat sarcastic sing-song tone.

Peter just shook his head. The guys in his old unit were masters at breaking tension with humor. Paul seemed like a good sport about it, which was a mark in his favor.

While they had been standing outside the circle, Mellie had been busy within. John and Urse had pulled up right behind them, and Urse had gone into the circle, without hesitation, to help her sister. She'd brought a bag full of stuff that kept the two women busy for a few minutes while John made a round of the guys who were heavily armed and visible around the circumference of the circle.

"Thanks for bringing the stuff, Urse, but now, you have to go." Mellie faced her sister, expecting an argument, but what she saw instead on her sister's face was resignation.

"I know, but I don't have to like it," Urse protested.

"Urse, you locked me in the apartment when it was your turn to cast spells," Mellie reminded her older sister.

"That was for your own protection!"

"Maybe so, but it was still a dirty trick," Mellie insisted, though she'd only just decided to forgive her sister for doing what she'd thought had been the right thing at the time. After the past few days, Mellie thought she understood Urse's decision a little better.

"I just wish I could help you more," Urse said, looking around the circle as if searching for something to do.

"You know you can't." Mellie went to Urse and took both of her hands in her own. "I probably shouldn't have let you come this far, but I miscalculated. I had no idea brewing this in town could be dangerous. I should have started out here from the beginning. Only a place like this can withstand the creation of something so powerful without affecting the physical world." Mellie let a bit of her worry come out in her words. "Even so, I'm concerned. There might be more tremors, or some other physical manifestation. I'm not really sure what to expect, which is why I don't want you here."

"I'm a big girl," Urse insisted. "I can take care of myself, and I promise not to interfere."

Mellie shot her a look that said it all. "If I were in danger, you know you'd be sticking your nose in where it doesn't belong, in a heartbeat. I love you, Urse, but you're a busybody. Nonna said neither of us could help the other in their task. You warded me into our apartment to prevent me from *helping*. I can't do the same to you, but I can appeal to your conscience. If Nonna said we have to do these things alone, we have to trust her."

Urse looked like she wanted to argue but knew she was wrong. She reached for Mellie and hugged her tight, emotion in every tight line of her body.

"I'll go, but I don't like it. I don't want to leave you all alone like this," Urse told her little sister, moving back slightly.

"I'm not alone," Mellie said softly. "Peter's here. You know he won't let anything hurt me. Not if he has anything to say about it. Just like John does for you."

"Huh." Urse looked from Mellie over to where Peter was standing just on the other side of the stones and back again. "I'm going to have to get used to you being mated to one of these big bear bruisers."

"Just like I got used to you snagging the Alpha of them all," Mellie replied, teasing her sister into a better humor.

"Yeah, but yours speaks dragon," Urse said, pointing to where Peter and Paul were talking in what sounded like Russian. Gus had left them to walk with John, and the two foreign-born shifters seemed to be bonding a bit.

Mellie laughed, just as Urse had intended.

CHAPTER FIFTEEN

Peter was intrigued to discover that the dragon shifter was fluent in Russian, even if his accent was of Moscow rather than Kamchatka. They were making small talk about the American bears and how Peter had gotten involved with the U.S. military unit after leaving Mother Russia for good, while they gave the sisters space to say goodbye. John hovered nearby, listening in. Paul probably didn't realize that most of the guys from the old unit were multilingual. Russian wasn't even the most difficult of the foreign languages some of them had mastered.

When Urse came out of the ring of stones, she had a tragic expression on her face. She was looking down as she walked away from her little sister, but when she reached John, she raised her gaze, and tears were streaking down her face as she sought the solace of her mate.

"I have to get out of here," Urse told John. "Nonna said each of our tasks must be performed alone. If I stay, I'll be tempted to interfere—especially if things get dangerous." Urse caught Peter's gaze. "You keep her safe, Peter. This thing could easily get out of her control. Or the leviathan could attack—we're not too far from the water here. Or any number of things. You have to be on guard." Urse sounded desperate.

"She is my life," he answered honestly. "Nothing will get to her. I will not allow it. And, if she looks to be in danger from the potion, I will pull her out, regardless of the consequences. I will not lose her after only just finding her." Peter tried to impress upon Urse the strength of his words, and she seemed to accept what he'd said. She nodded once and turned into John's loose embrace, allowing her mate to lead her away.

Which meant John wouldn't be on scene for the big show. Hmm. Problematic, but not too large a problem. Brody was here. He could coordinate the ground troops as easily as John. Even as he thought this, Brody appeared at his side.

"I'm taking the two-footed troops and will coordinate our fire," Brody said without preamble. "Gus is going bear and will wrangle those in fur. I suppose you two will be in the circle with Mellie?"

"Until the potion is done, then we have to get her to the water to deliver it," Peter explained as Brody frowned. "We're going down to the beach outside the ward to give the potion the best positioning to cover as much of the coast as possible. We'll need help getting there."

"If need be, I will take my other form," Paul surprised Peter by saying. "After last night, I have a score to settle with the leviathan, and I may be able to keep it far enough from shore to allow Mellie to do her work. You bears could work on protecting her from the smaller creatures," he offered, no disrespect in his tone, despite the offhanded nature of his words. They all knew the smaller creatures were nothing to trifle with.

"It's a good plan," Brody said after a moment's thought. "I'll go tell Gus the game plan, then we're ready to roll whenever you are."

"I suggest we do this soon because I believe the creatures have taken note of our activity," Paul said, gesturing toward the water, which was beginning to roil in an unnatural way.

"Shit," Peter's curse was echoed by Brody as he hustled away.

Mellie was just about ready to resume the brew. Urse had left, thankfully. Much as she loved her sister, this was something she had to do on her own. Just as Urse's task had been accomplished without any help from Mellie. Now that she was mated to Peter, she realized these two tasks were really a demarcation line in their lives.

When they'd been younger and learning the craft, they'd always done everything together. Urse usually led because she was the elder, but she and Mellie had learned together and practiced their art together. Later, as they'd begun to specialize, they'd still been there to help each other and watch each other's backs. But not this time.

These two tasks in Grizzly Cove had been the first time either of them had attempted such powerful magic on their own. Both had approached the task a single woman, and before they had completed their missions, each of them had become mated.

Had Nonna known what would happen? Mellie was close to one hundred percent certain her clairvoyant grandma had seen it all well ahead of time.

Now, it was Mellie's turn to unleash the magic she'd been born to wield. After a number of disheartening false starts, Mellie was ready now. She had the skill. She had done the preparation. And now, she had the right ingredients. The *secret ingredient*, if you will…a real live dragon shifter.

As the thought crossed her mind, the two men she was waiting for crossed into the circle. She had already gone around, consecrating the sacred space, clearing it of any residual energies. She would use the power of the stones to contain her creation until it was ready to be unleashed against the leviathan.

Goddess help them all.

"We'd better get a move on," Peter said, coming to her side. "The creatures grow restless."

Mellie looked out toward the water and cursed under her breath.

"Let's do this," she said, resolution in her tone, then she looked around for Paul. Spotting him, she gestured for the dragon shifter to come and stand at her side. "Are you ready to resume?" she asked him.

"Ready when you are. Just give me the signal," Paul told her. Peter was very impressed with the way the dragon shifter had stepped up so far.

Mellie began her chant again. This time, the words weren't deadened by the close confines of the furnished room in her apartment. No, this time, the stones echoed with the power of her chant. Peter felt the earth beneath his feet, singing with power in a low rumble that spoke to his shifter nature…his very soul.

Mellie had poured the potion into a golden chalice Urse must have brought with her. It had a wide brim and deep-set bowl on an ornate pedestal covered in runes, gems and glyphs of arcane power. The potion bubbled gently, a dark, almost opaque brown in color. As she chanted, it looked like the bubbling increased until, finally, she signaled to Paul.

It was time for the second drop of dragon shifter blood. Paul again pricked the third finger on his left hand and let a single drop of blood well up before inverting his finger over the chalice and allowing the blood drop to drip into the potion.

This time, in addition to the rumble of the earth, there was light within the circle of stones as a protective bubble rose around the circle, each stone adding light to meet at the center of the dome above their heads. Peter remained alert, watching every angle, searching for hidden dangers.

In the light coming off the ring of stones, the roiling ocean became even more visible. Peter didn't really need his superior night vision to see the tumult out at sea as hundreds—maybe thousands—of the evil sea creatures tangled together as they tried to get closer to shore. And, above them all, the massive tentacles of the leviathan waved threateningly.

Peter looked to Mellie, but she either didn't see it or didn't want to look and break her concentration. He then looked at Paul and saw his own concern was reflected on the dragon shifter's face. They would fight a battle trying to get this potion down to the water, and they both knew it.

Peter made the hand signal that he knew his friends outside the circle could see, even if they couldn't hear what was going on in the consecrated space. His signal said "get ready". Grim nods met his eyes as he looked at the men closest to him. They could see it, too…and probably hear it, as well.

Inside the circle of stones, they were protected from the sounds of the creatures. The churning of the water and the eerie screeches the leviathan had been known to make when communicating instructions to its minions. It probably sounded like something else underwater, but above the surface, it was like fingernails scratching on a blackboard. Or something equally evil.

Mellie chanted on, the potion now a translucent golden brown that was bubbling madly. Her words came to a peak, and she again nodded to Paul. He allowed another final drop of his blood to enter the chalice, and at that moment, the contents burst into a pure golden flame.

Peter reared back, unprepared for the violent reaction, but Mellie stood firm. She'd known, or perhaps had guessed, this might happen. Her beautiful face was lit by the glow of magic issuing from the flames in the chalice.

"It's done," she said. "Now, we just need to get this into the water. Quickly."

Peter surveyed the situation outside the circle. Though he couldn't hear it, he could see the telltale muzzle flashes as his comrades opened fire on the increasingly bold creatures. Some were even trying to crawl up the beach on dozens of tentacles and making surprisingly fast progress.

Peter's eyes widened. Up 'til now, they hadn't shown any tendencies to be amphibious, but who really knew what these evil things were capable of? They weren't from this realm of existence. For all anyone knew, they could fly.

Peter escorted Mellie and her glowing, flaming chalice to the edge of the circle closest to the shoreline. The moment they stepped over the boundary and outside the ring of stones, chaos reigned. The sound of the creatures screeching was deafening, as was the increasing barrage of gunfire. Even as they walked, the situation was intensifying.

Peter spotted Gus rallying the four-footed troops. "To me!" Peter called out, and a chorus of bear growls answered his call.

Foremost among them was a huge auburn female. Babushka had come to help.

Peter felt relief fill him. His babushka was probably the fiercest fighter of them all—and that was saying something. She had centuries of experience and cunning, and she was larger than almost all of the other bears. Babushka was formidable.

The bears formed a row facing outward, battling the smaller creatures that dared come up on land while providing a safe passageway for Peter and Mellie. Paul had stopped at the head of the column and started shedding his clothing. If Peter wasn't very much mistaken, they were all about to see a real live dragon in action.

He felt the wind buffet him as the dragon took to the air behind them, but Peter remained focused on his mission. Getting Mellie and her precious chalice to the water was the most important thing right now. Everyone else was there to support them in that goal, and he would not waste their efforts or sacrifice.

Around him, he heard the barrage of gunfire, and one enterprising ex-military guy had even brought along a rocket launcher. He was throwing fire with that every few minutes, when he had a good target. The leviathan's minions were being engaged on all fronts, but there were just too many of them.

In the latest explosion of rocket fire, Peter looked up to see the outline of a massive dragon winging its way over the water.

"Holy shit, that's a fucking dragon!" Peter heard one of his comrades in two-legged form call out over the noise of the ongoing gunfire.

"Don't shoot him," Brody roared back. "He's on our side."

And, just like that, the guns aimed to help the dragon, whose midsection began to glow eerily. A moment later, fire erupted in the sky, heading for the shoreline, illuminating the nightmare scene of thousands of tentacles crawling their way up the beach, heading for the defenders. Peter felt his heart stutter, just for a second. Then, he saw the effect the dragon fire had on the creatures.

They ran. In some cases, climbing over each other in their efforts to get away. Those that didn't escape the flames, sort of… melted. And many died.

Peter realized that those that had been created of this earth were killable around the same time the rest of the guys did, and after that, they seemed to have new purpose. Not all those minions had come through from another plane of existence. It was clear now that many had been made here—earth creatures formed into hideous monsters by the leviathan's twisted magic. They could be killed, and the men and bears on the beach redoubled their efforts.

Peter had his arm around Mellie as the bears closed ranks around them. The small strip of rocky sand leading down the beach that the bears guarded began to shrink as battle intensified, but the dragon's repeated fire helped prevent anything from crawling up from the water between the ranks of bears.

Babushka was down there too, at the end of the column, two white bears flanking her—one was Sven, the town's doctor and only resident polar bear. The other was Gus, the shaman and rare spirit bear. Both were immensely powerful.

Between the three of them, nothing was getting between the two lines of bears.

Mellie guarded that chalice as best she could. The fire within heated the gold of the cup, but it didn't harm her. It was a magical fire that would burn itself out within a few minutes if she didn't use the potion right away. The highest potency of this particular potion was just after it was brewed. It would still be quite magical corked in a bottle a hundred years from now, but in order to do the most good, it had to be fresh.

Her job right now was to get it into the water as soon as possible.

The earth began to shake beneath her feet, threatening her balance, and she thought for a moment the potion had stirred an earthquake. As Peter steadied her, his strong arm around her waist, she realized the leviathan was causing the shaking. It was sending its heavy, muscular tentacles, thundering down on the sandy bottom of the ocean floor and partway onto the beach itself, crushing some of its minions that happened to be in the way of its wrath. It was trying to reach the bears, but they were fast enough to scramble out of the way. Thank the Goddess.

But Mellie realized she was going to have to get closer than she ever wanted to get to that creature and its crushing, flailing arms. Water was splashing everywhere, and the bears closest to the shore were half-in-half-out of the waves the leviathan was churning up with its frenzy. She was so afraid someone was going to get killed. She couldn't have that on her conscience.

Part of her wanted to run as fast as she could down to the water, but the chalice was wide-brimmed and she dared not lose a single drop of the precious potion. She had to just calm down.

"You can do this," she told herself, giving herself the quiet pep talk that had helped her when she was first learning how to condense her magic down into liquid form.

"I'm right with you," Peter added. That was new. Always before, she'd faced the danger of her own power—and anything that came against her magically—with her sister backing her up. Or sometimes, their grandmother. Never a man. This would take some getting used to.

Urse's power to cast spells was something that could be done on the fly. As a result, she was better at dealing with immediate threats. Potions took more finesse…and more time. Which was why Mellie had always been tasked with the more long-term problems.

Never in her life could Mellie have imagined this scenario. She'd usually done her work from the shadows, with the luxury of time. This time, she was on the front lines, in the direct path of danger. Without Peter at her side, she honestly didn't know if she would've had the courage to continue. The leviathan was scary!

"Don't let it get to you," Peter shouted to be heard above the screeching and gunfire, not to mention the dragon's roaring flame. "The creature is projecting fear. It bounces off us bears, but some of it might get through to you. Fight it, Mellie!"

Just hearing Peter's words broke the spell. Mellie shook her head once and cursed. That damned leviathan had many tricks up its metaphorical sleeve. Mellie should have been more aware that it could try to trick her. It had done its best to lure Urse away from the protection of her own wards, after all.

"Thank you, Peter," Mellie shouted as they kept moving. Her feet were no longer hesitant. The fear that had almost disabled her, moments before, was a thing of the past.

Oh, sure, she was apprehensive about getting too close to the water and the creature within it that wanted her power, but she wasn't crippled by debilitating fear. No. Mellie wasn't going to play the leviathan's game. Not by its rules.

It was time to level the playing field and destroy the competition.

With purposeful strides, Mellie walked as quickly as she

could without spilling a drop of her potion. The bears on either side growled in combat, giving of themselves and their immense strength to protect her on this dangerous promenade.

Mellie began to chant, invoking the protections of the Goddess that all *strega* knew. To her amazement, little tendrils of golden flame licked out of the sides of the chalice to aid the bears who were fighting for their lives to protect Mellie on her walk. She hadn't expected that, but it was welcome. Every little bit helped.

As she drew closer to the water, the glowing fire spilling out of the chalice intensified. It formed a shield of protection around her and Peter, who remained at her side. Granny Ivana was fighting alongside a massive polar bear and a strange cream-colored bear that must be Gus. They were going tooth and claw against the sea creatures, half in the water as it sprayed high in the tumult.

"I need to get into the water," Mellie said to Peter, breaking her chant. There had to be a way to deliver her potion without getting killed, but she wasn't sure how.

The chalice of potion was providing some protection, but she also wasn't sure if that shield was impenetrable. The potion hadn't really been designed to do what it was now doing. She had to get it into the water, a few feet from shore. Only once it mixed with the water of the coastline could it take full effect.

"Follow me," Peter shouted. He'd taken off his clothes and flung them back the way they'd come. In an instant of shimmering energy, he shifted into his bear form and moved in front of her.

Mellie understood what he was trying to do. He was placing himself between her and danger. She would not waste his efforts, though she intended to have strong words with him after this was all over. She didn't like seeing him in danger any more than he probably enjoyed watching her do this.

Moving quickly, she held the chalice aloft and walked

boldly into the splash zone. It was so chaotic on the shore that she wasn't exactly certain where the water normally began. She had to go in up to her knees, at least, to be certain the potion would disperse to the widest possible area.

Peter slashed out in front of her, his claws coming back slicked in blood and gore, though in the darkness she couldn't see it all that well. The night was lit with occasional bursts of dragon fire and the diminishing fire of rockets and grenades. Muzzle flashes moved closer on either side of the line of bears, aiming out to sea, but for a human mage with no real night vision, it was still pretty dark.

Mellie felt water on her lower legs and feared any moment she would feel the sting of suckers or teeth, but she had to keep going. Step by step, the water became deeper, and she finally became convinced that she was in the tidal zone.

She chanted her last incantation and raised the chalice high in front of her. Then, she did as she'd been praying she'd get a chance to do and poured the chalice out into the water directly in front of her.

The change was almost instantaneous. The glowing golden flames spread like wildfire, and the cacophony of dying evil rose high in the night air. The immediate area around her became a writhing mass of flame that consumed only evil. The defenders basked in the goodness of the glowing magic that healed any injuries they had sustained in this battle, and refreshed their souls.

The leviathan and its minions were not so lucky. The smaller ones dissolved in bursts of golden fire. The larger ones fled as fast as they could, and the largest of all—the leviathan itself—screamed in outrage as it was pushed back with incredible force on a tidal wave of golden flame.

CHAPTER SIXTEEN

Peter had never experienced anything like the magical fire that issued from Mellie's golden chalice. It burned the creatures to a crisp but washed over the defenders harmlessly. He was able to stand back and watch its progress as the potion mixed incredibly fast with the ocean waters.

It licked down the coast in both directions and as far out to sea as he could see with his naked eye. He actually saw the leviathan lifted up by a golden wave of power and thrown—there was no better word for it—over the horizon. Or, at least, as much of the horizon as a bear shifter could see in the dark illuminated only by the golden magic of Mellie's potion.

The dragon was last seen flying out after the leviathan, and Peter wasn't sure if Paul was just enraged enough to follow the creature and continue the fight or if he was merely doing reconnaissance. Ushering the evil thing away from land, as it were. Once and for all.

At least...Peter hoped it was once and for all. If Mellie's potion worked as well as her sister's wards, then the leviathan had just been banished from a good portion of the Pacific coast of the US, Canada and maybe as far as Mexico. He'd have to reach out to the shifter grapevine tomorrow to see just how far Mellie's protections extended.

Pride filled his heart for his clever mate. Peter turned to look at her, just in time to watch her collapse onto her knees in the surf. In a flash, he was back in his human form, and he caught her in his arms, cradling her close.

Where the beach before had been dominated by a cacophony of sound, it was now silent. The only sounds were the welcome snuffles of bears and the familiar clicks of weaponry standing down.

Babushka came over in her bear form and chuffed at Mellie's hair—a tender sign of care and concern among bears of the same Clan. He knew what his grandmother was saying without words.

Care for your mate. She did very well. Things along those lines. Approval and love from the ancient bear that touched Peter deeply. If his babushka accepted his mate, Mellie would be welcome in his home Clan. She was already accepted among his adopted Clan with the bears of Grizzly Cove, but it meant a lot to Peter to have his grandmother's welcome for his mate, as well.

Lifting Mellie into his arms, he carried her away from the battlefield. Others would finish up here. Now was the time to look to his own and make certain his mate was safe and secure.

"Did it work?" Mellie asked weakly as he walked out of the once-again gentle surf, holding her securely in his arms.

"Like a charm, *zvyozdochka,*" he told her. "You were magnificent." He placed a gentle kiss on her hair. "Rest now. I will take care of you," he crooned, walking past everyone and everything, heading for his truck. "You've done an amazing thing here tonight, my love."

Mellie was asleep by the time he buckled her into the passenger seat of his vehicle. Zak had trotted up, holding Peter's discarded clothing out to him.

"Your lady done good," Zak said by way of greeting.

Peter accepted the clothes and slid into his pants and

boots. The upholstery on his seat was scratchy enough to warrant a bit of protection, but he just chucked the shirt into the backseat. He didn't want to waste too much time in getting his mate home to their den.

"She is one in a million," Peter agreed, his voice going soft. "Thank you for your help tonight. Pass the word to the rest," Peter said seriously, taking a brief moment to put his hand on Zak's shoulder. "Never have I been prouder to call you all comrades," he said.

Zak nodded. "We're Clan," he said simply, and they both knew the bonds they shared were stronger than that of mere family. The core group of bear shifters that had formed around John and founded Grizzly Cove had chosen each other as brothers. They'd fought alongside each other for decades and forged bonds that would never be broken.

Zak stepped back. "You'll have an escort shortly, and your granny already claimed a ride back to your place in the Jeep with the fifty-cal on top. She's quite a lady."

Peter had to laugh. The bears of Grizzly Cove had no idea what Babushka could get up to, but tonight, they just might have started to get an inkling. He hoped his grandmother would decide to stay. He loved having her around, and she could teach these American bears a thing or two. Peter would truly enjoy watching such a thing.

Peter drove down from the point and headed straight for his den. There were escort vehicles before and after his truck, and they waited while he pulled into his drive, several bears materializing out of the forest to check the perimeter for Peter while he dealt with his sleeping mate. The Clan was pulling out all the stops to protect and show their deep respect for what Mellie had done tonight. Peter was touched by their concern and glad to have the guys from the old unit helping to secure his home tonight.

Peter knew he was too preoccupied with Mellie's condition, at the moment, to be as thorough as he usually was with security checks. Evil had been running amok not too far away, and it was simply good policy to be certain his home hadn't been tampered with while they were battling evil elsewhere.

A half dozen bears made short work of the perimeter check, and Zak got out of one of the escort vehicles to help Peter go through the interior of the house before he took Mellie inside. All was as he had left it earlier, and there had been no breaches, but it was still good to check and kind of his teammates to take the time to help.

He saw them off with a friendly wave, knowing some of the guys in bear form would station themselves in the woods around his property for the remainder of the night. That was their way. When one of the unit was down for any reason, the others automatically helped pick up the slack.

Mellie was down—at least for a while—and the others were responding. Their actions said, louder than words, that they had already accepted her as part of the team. She was one of them now, for certain. She had proved herself in every way tonight, and her willingness to face danger in order to protect innocents had won them over completely.

Zak put Mellie in his bed, stripping off her wet clothing and wiping down her legs with a damp washcloth to remove the salt water residue. She would probably want to take a shower later, but he didn't have a heart to wake her up at the moment. The wipe down would have to suffice for now.

He then went into the living room to call Urse. Peter knew Brody would already have reported back to John on the events of the evening, but he also suspected Mellie would want him to talk to her sister, to reassure Urse that Mellie really was okay.

Urse asked a lot of questions, and Peter answered to the best of his ability, staying on the phone with Mellie's sister far longer than he'd anticipated. Finally, John took the phone from his mate and gave Peter the sit rep. Early reports of the potion's dispersal were good.

Urse had received a call from the girls' grandmother in San Francisco at almost the same moment the potion had been unleashed. The old woman had felt the magic where she lived and called to pass on her impressions. According to Nonna Ricoletti, the potion was far stronger than even she had expected, and she wouldn't be surprised—in her words—if the effects stretched as far south as Mexico. She would call friends along the coast in the morning to see if she could get a more accurate assessment.

John also had feelers out to other shifter groups along the coast for exactly the same reason. All indications were that Mellie had outdone herself. She'd protected not only Grizzly Cove, but far up and down the coast, as well. Just how far her magic had spread remained to be seen, but things were really looking good according to what John had been able to piece together so far.

He had one final bit of advice to pass on from his mate before they ended the call. Urse warned Peter not to worry if Mellie should sleep for a dozen hours or more. Her potions took a lot out of her sometimes, Urse explained, and if this one was as powerful as it seemed, Mellie would likely need a bit of time to recover.

Peter hung up the phone and thought about what he could do to make Mellie's rest easier. She was as clean as he could make her and propped up by soft pillows on his bed. He would hold her for the rest of the night, once he was free to seek his bed, but at the moment, he wanted to wait up to talk to his grandmother. He knew she was getting a ride back on the gun truck, so she wouldn't be far behind.

As he stood there, thinking about his next move, he heard the unmistakable sound of the heavily armed Jeep pulling up in front of his house. A few moments later, his grandmother entered through the front door, grinning happily as she waved goodbye to Peter's comrades.

"You're certainly fitting in well with my friends," Peter observed, moving forward to meet his babushka. He opened his arms, and they hugged each other for a long moment.

"Your friends are a lot of fun," Babushka told Peter with a grin as she moved away. "I can see why you decided to stay here with them rather than return to Kamchatka, though I was upset with your choice at first. Now, I see the wisdom of it. Here, you had the chance of finding your mate and forging a new life among bears who were your brothers, though not of our Clan. You've made your own Clan among these strange bears, and although I did not understand how such a thing could work before seeing it myself, it is a healthy family. A place where much happiness is possible."

Neither of them had to speak the sad truth that the Clan back on Kamchatka was dwindling and somewhat inbred. There had been no females there that had ever really spiked Peter's interest. He'd known early on that he'd have to find a mate outside his familial territory, which had been a large part of the appeal of joining the military and traveling the world in the first place.

"I am happy here, Babushka. Mellie makes me happy," Peter said simply.

"I can see that," she replied, smiling and cupping Peter's cheek fondly. "I believe I will stay here for a while. The Clan back home is in good shape, and I want to learn more of your American bears and watch your mate learn her way in this new Clan. I want to be here to help you both, especially if there is any babysitting that needs doing in the near future." Babushka chuckled as Peter felt shock run through him. He hadn't really thought that far ahead yet to cubs.

Still chuckling, she walked away toward the back of the house and the room Peter had designed into the layout with her in mind. He'd decorated it in her favorite colors and had kept it ready should she ever decide to visit. He was happy to have her here, and the fact that she'd decided to stay for a while filled his heart with joy.

"I love you, Babushka," he said quietly, knowing she heard him.

She paused and blew a kiss back at him, then went on her way to her room.

*

Mellie stretched, finding herself naked in Peter's bed. There was no window in the room, so she couldn't really tell whether it was day or night, but a clock on the night stand read 4:27. She looked at the open doorway and thought she detected light coming down the hall, but that didn't really tell her whether it was a.m. or p.m. She'd have to get up and investigate.

Rising, she realized the bed was mussed on both sides, as if Peter had been holding her while she slept. Just the thought of him sent warmth through her heart, love causing her to sigh with happiness. He must've taken care of her after she passed out on the beach.

He'd also left clothing near the foot of the bed for her. Soft sweatpants and a T-shirt from her own wardrobe. Maybe Urse had brought some of her clothes over because Mellie didn't think Peter would have left her alone for long while she was unconscious. Not judging by the way newly mated bear shifters behaved with their mates.

She grabbed the clothing and went into the attached bathroom, opting for a quick shower to make her feel more human. When she was done, the fresh clothes felt soft against her skin as she did her best to figure out how long she'd slept.

Mellie stumbled out into the hallway and followed her nose toward the smell of coffee. She found Peter and his grandmother sitting at the kitchen table, talking quietly in Russian. They both smiled when the saw her, and Peter stood, coming over to her and giving her a kiss in greeting.

"How are you feeling?" he asked, searching her eyes as he pulled back from the kiss that was altogether too short.

"Better. How long did I sleep?"

"Almost twenty-nine hours. You had me worried, but Urse came over yesterday and checked on you a couple of times. She said you were just sleeping it off and convinced me not to worry," Peter told her. She could see in his eyes that he *had* been worried, despite Urse's reassurances.

"Oh, wow. I've never slept that long after a casting. I think my previous record was like twenty-two hours, but that only happened one time, when I was first learning to do the really intense potions." She did her best to sound casual about the whole thing. She didn't want to worry him more, but the fact that she'd lost a whole day kind of freaked her out. "I'm kind of hungry. I guess I'm too late for lunch and too early for dinner." She looked around the house, trying to change the subject to something more mundane and less touchy.

"In a shifter house, there is always food," Granny Ivana said, reappearing at the kitchen table with a plate of sandwiches in her hand. "Come. Sit. You must eat while we tell you the results of your work."

The sandwiches were just about calling her name, so Mellie took Granny Ivana's words to heart. "Thank you so much," Mellie told the older woman. "I guess I missed quite a few meals while I was recovering."

"A whole day and more," Granny Ivana agreed. "Start with this, and then, we'll see what else you might want."

"If I eat all these sandwiches, I'll explode," Mellie joked, laughing as she selected a turkey and cheese sandwich off the platter. She took a bite before curiosity got the better of her. "What did you say about the results of the potion?"

She was eager to know what changes that amazing potion had wrought. Mellie was fairly certain the potion had done something truly spectacular, but she hadn't been able to stay conscious long enough to really see what had happened.

"The data is still coming in, but Paul flew after the leviathan, watching it get literally thrown from the shoreline faster than the dragon could fly," Peter told her. "I'm still not totally sure what drove Paul to follow the creature—whether it was rage or merely curiosity—but either way, he chased it a good ten miles out to sea."

"Ten miles?" Mellie almost choked on her sandwich. Even she hadn't expected that kind of range.

"It seems pretty uniform," Peter said, nodding. "Paul flew out last night to see if he could gather more information, and he said it looked like the creatures have been pushed back roughly the same distance as far as he could fly up and down the shoreline. He went south first, until the increased shipping traffic heading for the larger California ports made him wary of being seen, then he headed north, all the way up to the Bering Sea. It seems your potion cut off the Bering Strait completely. The leviathan and its little friends can't access the Strait and a good portion of the major fishing grounds in the Bering Sea, which is excellent news for the commercial fishing industry."

Mellie chewed and swallowed mechanically, shocked by what she was hearing. That potion had done even more than she'd suspected.

"And there's more," Granny Ivana chimed in, smiling like a cat who had swallowed the proverbial canary. "I called the family in Kamchatka," she went on, drawing her news out for full effect. "Your potion shot up the North American Pacific Coast, up to the Bering Sea and across to Russia. You have protected a large swath of Siberia and the Kamchatka Peninsula. You have protected my homeland with the same ten-mile safety zone into the ocean."

"Unbelievable," Mellie murmured, amazed by the news.

"Believe it," Granny Ivana went on. "The effect diminishes somewhat after leaving Kamchatka's shores. Japan received some protection, but not quite at the same level."

"We're still working on getting the data from the southward expansion, but early reports seem to indicate the same kind of safety zone extending from Grizzly Cove, southward to about the Panama Canal," Peter added.

"Wow." Mellie gave up all pretense of eating. She was truly shocked at the power of the potion. "I mean, I thought it would be potent, but I had no idea it would go that far, or that deep into the ocean. Have the mer checked it out?"

"First thing this morning," Peter confirmed, smiling broadly. "They can leave the cove for the first time in a long time. They're so happy they want to throw a party in your honor."

It was a lot to take in. She remembered being concerned

about the golden flame, and she also remembered seeing it shoot down the shoreline as if an oil slick had caught on fire. Only, it wasn't a normal flame. It was a magical fire that was almost translucent and glowing. Not normal-looking at all.

"What about the flame? Did you all see it?" she asked.

"We saw it," Granny Ivana confirmed, "but apparently, it was invisible to non-magical folk. Otherwise, there might have been quite a commotion."

"And the tremors? The earth was shaking, wasn't it?" Mellie asked, trying to piece together the disjointed recollections in her mind. The potion had taken the vast majority of her attention, but she'd been aware of what was going on around her in a peripheral way.

"It wasn't an earthquake. Using the stone circle contained the power of the potion nicely," Peter told her. "The shaking you felt as you dashed for the water came from the leviathan pounding its tentacles on the ocean floor. That's also what caused the big waves. John and your sister didn't feel any tremors in town, and no earthquakes were reported for that time anywhere in the ring of fire."

"That's a relief," Mellie said, sighing. "I was afraid I might have caused earthquakes with that potion. I've never handled anything so powerful before."

"Well, you did it masterfully," Peter told her, leaning in to place a kiss on her temple. "Finish your sandwich," he scolded with a happy grin. "I'll call your sister to tell her you're awake. She made me promise to call."

"Sounds like Urse." Mellie laughed and picked up the second half of her sandwich and began to eat it.

She felt truly happy and filled with relief for the first time since the task of brewing a protective potion for Grizzly Cove had been given to her. She had accomplished her task. Finally. It hadn't been easy, and it hadn't been quick, but she'd done it. Thank the Mother of All.

CHAPTER SEVENTEEN

Peter kept a watchful eye on Mellie for the next few hours as her sister arrived to check on her. John had come with his mate, and the men gave the sisters space to hug and discuss magical stuff. At one point, the sisters called their grandmother, using the teleconferencing setup in Peter's study while John, Peter and his Babushka—or Granny Ivana as she was becoming known in Grizzly Cove—sat in the living room.

"I'm so glad you've decided to stay for a while," John told Peter's grandmother.

"Your town intrigues me," she replied. "Frankly, I didn't see how it could work when Peter described it to me, but now that I'm here, I'm very impressed. And you know, I make dolls."

John seemed a little stymied by what seemed to be a rather odd observation, but Peter knew what his babushka was getting at. He tried not to laugh at John's attempts to hide his confusion.

"Nesting dolls," Peter added, trying to help…but not too much. John still looked confused, but doing his best to hide it, and Peter burst out laughing. "Russian nesting dolls are a work of *art*," Peter said and watched the light bulb go off.

"Oh! Art." John seemed to have finally comprehended what she was trying to say. The cover for the town was that they were an artists' colony, after all. "What do you need for a studio, Granny Ivana?"

"I was thinking maybe Peter could help me build a little space next to his shop. I don't want a full-fledged gallery, but a little workshop with a space in front for display and sales would work nicely and wouldn't take too long to construct."

Peter wasn't surprised his babushka had it all planned out. The woman was born making plans, and everyone just followed along. It was easier that way. And her plans were good.

"I already have your cousin sending out some of my finished pieces that haven't sold yet," she went on to tell Peter. She turned back to John. "I'll be sending some of the money home," she told the Alpha bear. "I've helped support the Clan with my dolls for a long time, but I've taught my craft to several others, and they can pick up production to keep the Clan running. It'll just take a little time for them to catch up. Until they do, I'm going to send part of my sales from here to them since I'm taking my reserved stock from them."

"I have no objection," John was quick to say. "The profits from any sales of art are yours to do with as you please. Most of our core group donates a portion of their sales to the town fund, but that's purely optional, and, as I said, it's something my old unit did on their own, not a requirement."

"Good." She nodded in that regal way she had. "I will give ten percent to the town fund and twenty to my home Clan for the first six months. After that, I will reassess."

Six months? Peter was overjoyed at the length of time his grandmother was contemplating. He had no idea she wanted to stay half a year or more. This was great news, and he felt his heart expand with joy.

"Can they spare you that long?" Peter asked in a low tone,

touched that she'd want to stay with him for any length of time.

She sighed heavily. "To be honest, the Clan needs a shake up. For too long, they've followed my lead without thinking for themselves. This will be good for them. And it makes way for the younger generation to take charge," she admitted, then smiled a soft smile, her old eyes sparkling. "You may have noticed, but I have a rather commanding personality."

Both men chuckled at her statement. "I think that's why we get along so well," Peter told her. "But I think I understand."

John was all smiles. "You are very welcome here," he told her formally. "You may have noticed that we have a lack of female influence. We have a lot of very strong personalities, but we've built up mutual respect in the years we've worked together. I think, in another situation, having this many bears with Alpha personalities in one place could easily be a recipe for disaster, but our core group worked out our dominance issues long ago, and we're all working toward the same goal here. We want to make happy lives for ourselves among friends. We want to stop traveling the world like vagabonds fighting other peoples' wars. We want peace and serenity, joy and laughter. We want mates. Some of us have been blessed to find them here. The rest have hope that their mates will be found soon. In the meantime, we want to create as normal a place as we can together, where we can be bears in the wild, when we need to, and have a safe place to walk among humans and make a living without having to kill people or put our own lives on the line." John paused, his expression earnest. "I think you'd fit in here very well, Mrs. Zilakov. We need female bears here to help balance us out. You might find that you fit into the role of granny to the whole town, if you give my guys the least indication that you're willing to give them advice or an ear to listen."

She nodded. "It would be my honor," she replied, her tone respectful. "I am babushka to my Clan, but they don't really need me. They are stable and content. In fact, by staying in Kamchatka, I'm probably hindering the younger generation from developing fully. But here… I could do some good here." Her smile reappeared.

*

After talking to her sister, and having a long conference with Nonna, Mellie was feeling more grounded. By all accounts, she'd managed an incredible feat with the potion and had protected more innocents with a single magical work than had been done in recent history. She'd also unearthed what could be the last dragon shifter in existence, but that news wasn't really for public consumption. Urse had told her the boys in town had called a meeting yesterday with Paul and given solemn oaths that word of his existence would go no farther.

Paul had, in turn, asked for permission to stay in the area, shocking the bears. They'd quickly conferred and given him the rundown on the purpose of the town and the local code of behavior. He'd agreed not to run amok in his dragon form across the countryside—only half joking, it seemed, or so a few of the bears had thought—and rented a room at the hotel at the end of the strip, pending further developments.

After her sandwich, Mellie had felt a lot better, though an hour later, she was hungry again. Urse and John urged her, Peter and his granny to come into town. Zak was holding a shindig at his restaurant to celebrate the momentous events and would be serving up a Cajun feast the likes of which hadn't been seen in Grizzly Cove before. Everyone was attending, from the new dragon to the youngest mer child… Or so they claimed.

Mellie didn't feel like a raucous party, but then again, it would be churlish of her to not attend. Plus, she was really hungry, and she loved Zak's cooking. She agreed to at least show her face and have a little food.

That turned into a four-hour appearance, during which time, multiple mer came up to her and thanked her for cleansing the ocean to such a magnificent extent. She hadn't really realized how trapped the mer had felt, confined to just the waters of the cove these past few months, but she thought she understood them better now.

The party wasn't all that raucous as she'd feared. Mostly, it was just big groups of friends sharing a meal with humorous conversation and good cheer. She enjoyed herself immensely and put away more of Zak's famous Cajun cooking than she would have believed. Then again, she was making up for a lost day, and food was fuel to many magical folk.

Nobody raised an eyebrow, and she felt more welcome in Grizzly Cove than she ever had before. They were celebrating her successful completion of the potion, but they were also rejoicing in her mating with Peter. When Peter announced that Granny Ivana would be staying and opening a workshop, there was a big cheer as well. Granny Ivana had impressed the fighting men of Grizzly Cove, and Mellie suspected she would definitely wind up being granny to the entire town.

As the evening wore down, Mellie started to feel fatigued again. That potion had taken a lot out of her, and she'd require a bit more sleep before she would fully recover. In fact, she might be weak for a while—as had happened to her sister after casting those permanent wards over the town and cove. But it was okay. Peter would take care of her.

"Why don't we stay in my apartment tonight?" she suggested, very much afraid that she would fall asleep before they made it back to Peter's den.

"If that's what you want," he answered easily, then, seeing how tired she was, he made their goodbyes and ushered her the short distance to the bookshop, carrying her up the stairs and putting her in bed.

She was unconscious before he joined her after locking up.

The next morning, Mellie woke feeling a lot better. The camaraderie and excellent food last night, in addition to a comfortable sleep, had helped restore her a bit more. Peter was in the apartment. She just knew it somehow. Maybe her senses were more attuned to him now that they were an acknowledged couple, or something.

Or maybe it was all the noise he was making. Was he *trying* to wake her up? She considered that thought a moment and wondered if that wasn't so far from the truth. Getting out of bed, she got clothes out of her dresser and headed for the bathroom. On the way, she saw Peter looking somewhat sheepish as he hustled down the hallway with a broom.

"What's going on?" she called after him, but he didn't stop.

"Nothing," he called back and disappeared into the kitchen. "Take your shower. I'm making breakfast. It'll be ready by the time you're done."

Shaking her head, she figured he'd looked okay to her. He probably hadn't gotten into anything dangerous in her cupboards. She'd give him the nickel tour of her potion cabinet later. If they were going to live together, he'd need to learn about the hazards of living with a potion witch.

As the sound of breaking glass and cursing in Russian and several other languages came from the other end of the hallway, she just moved on toward the bathroom. She'd deal with it when she was dressed—and had shoes on to protect her bare feet from the glass.

Looked like Peter was taking a crash course this morning, she thought, snickering to herself as she went into the bathroom.

Once everything had been cleaned up, and Peter had been given the grand tour of what to touch and what to leave alone in the kitchen, they ate a sumptuous breakfast of chocolate chip pancakes. Apparently, it had been the search for the mini chips that had predicated Peter's somewhat disastrous acquaintance with the contents of two special cupboards Mellie reserved just for her potions.

She didn't mind. He was okay, and she could easily replace the common potions he'd disturbed. He wasn't to know that some of her concoctions wouldn't take kindly to being moved without her approval, but he was learning fast. She was sure there were probably things about living with a shifter that she'd have to get used to, but she looked forward to it. She had a future, now, that was quite different from her past, and she couldn't wait to embark on the life she and Peter would live together.

Urse came up from the shop to visit for a bit and make sure Mellie was all right. She refused to let Mellie work in the shop at all that day, insisting that she continue to rest.

"Sis, I know what casting those wards took out of me. Your potion was the equivalent of that and more," Urse told her in a no-nonsense tone. "Your main job now is to rest and recover. Relax for a bit with your mate. Let him take care of you and just concentrate on getting your energy back. It won't happen overnight, but the more you take it easy, the faster it will happen."

"I don't like it, but you've talked me into being a couch potato," Mellie told her older sister.

Urse bent down to kiss her sister on the forehead before she headed out of the apartment and back to the shop. "Rest up. Pete…" Urse addressed Peter, who was hovering in the kitchen, cleaning up again. "Keep an eye on this one. No working at all today. Don't even let her think about setting foot in her potion room."

"I'll make it my top priority," Peter promised, his expression overly serious.

Mellie threw a decorative pillow off the couch at him. He fielded it easily and hung on to it as he came out of the kitchen area. He had an intent look in his eyes.

"On that note…" Urse left them, heading back down the stairs with a big grin on her face.

Mellie saw that her sister had closed and locked the door behind herself.

As Peter advanced on the couch on which Mellie was sitting, he tossed the pillow aside, his gaze never leaving hers. Mellie knew that look now. It started a little fire of delight inside her, knowing the pleasure it portended.

"You want to play, my little mate? I'll give you something to play with," he told her, his voice dropping low. He really was the sexiest man on Earth. Hands down.

"Promises, promises," she retorted, loving the little growl that escaped him as he lowered himself to the couch, taking her to a prone position in one smooth move.

Then, his lips were on hers, and she didn't come to her senses again for some time. Peter lay over her, warm and inviting. She ran her hands over his muscular body as he undressed them both. He was so perfect for her, so strong and caring. How had she gotten so lucky, or so blessed, to get a man like this in her life?

She wasn't sure how it had happened, but she was clear on one point. She would keep him in her life, and in her bed, for the rest of her days. There was no uncertainty about that. No thought that things might not work out or that the flame of desire they felt now might some day diminish. No. What they had was real, and lasting. It would stand the test of time. That, she knew, deep in her heart.

This was forever.

Peter joined his body to hers, pausing once he was deep inside to look down into her eyes. Time stood still as the day went on around them, oblivious to the two lovers locked in each other's embrace.

"I love you, my *zvyozdochka*. Now and forever," Peter told her, stealing her heart all over again.

"I love you, too, Peter, but if you don't start moving in the next three seconds, I may have to zap you," she teased.

"Zap?" His brow quirked, even as he chuckled.

Mellie called a little wisp of magical energy into existence, cradling it in her hand. She brought it between them to make sure he saw it. When his eyes widened, she flicked it at him, and he jumped as the tiny zap of magic hit him on the shoulder. It didn't hurt. At least, she hadn't intended it to hurt. He looked more surprised than anything else.

"That tickled," he accused in a tone full of wonder. "I didn't know you could manifest magical energy that way."

"A woman likes to have a few secrets, you know," she told him, smiling up at him, even as she squirmed, squeezing him with her internal muscles.

He growled, and she did it again. "I think I'm going to enjoy living with a witch. You've definitely put a spell on me that I never want to break."

"Goes both ways," Mellie gasped as Peter began a hard, thrusting rhythm. Oh, yeah. That's just what she'd wanted.

She came almost immediately, but Peter wasn't letting her off that easy. He lifted her in his arms, still riding his cock, and walked them down the hall to her bedroom. The walking motion and the resulting stimulation roused her once again, and when he lay back on her bed, she took the top position.

She came twice more before he joined her in ecstasy. Then, they showered together and made love once more against the tiles of her shower, then again with her butt perched on the bathroom vanity. It was as if they were making up for lost time, or something.

Mellie wasn't exactly sure what prompted the sexual frenzy, but she wasn't going to question it too closely. This time was for enjoying her new mate, not deep thinking about causation.

Although... It might've been the danger, or the fact that she'd been unconscious for so long. Perhaps, he'd been worried about her. Maybe that's why he was so eager to please her—and himself—right now. Or maybe it was just the normal thing that happened to bear shifters when the found their mates. Whatever had caused the marathon of ecstasy, Mellie wasn't going to complain. Not at all.

Then, a thought occurred to her. What if it was just Peter? What if she was truly the luckiest woman in the world and her mate was the most gifted lover she would ever know?

What if the perfection of their union was something reserved for them alone? Perhaps it was this way for every shifter who found their true mate. That would explain why they were so keen to find the one partner meant only for them.

Yeah, that could very well be it. Mellie sent up a prayer of thanks to the Mother of All for sending her the perfect man for her as he carried her back to the bed and started making love to her all over again.

CHAPTER EIGHTEEN

Peter and Mellie returned to his den for the night. They were having dinner with Granny Ivana. She'd called the apartment to make certain they were coming back to the den, so they had to get cleaned up and presentable for dinner with Granny, whether they liked it or not. But humoring Granny Ivana wasn't a hardship. Mellie was pleased that the older woman was so accepting.

Mellie had feared Peter's relatives would object to having a witch in the family. As it was, Granny Ivana couldn't have been friendlier if she tried. Mellie finally arrived at the conclusion that Granny Ivana just wanted to see Peter happy and was willing to accept that Mellie made him feel that way.

So, they showed up for dinner right on time, ready to enjoy an evening with the woman who was fast becoming the town's favorite grandmother. When they arrived, however, Granny Ivana was not alone. She had invited Paul to dinner, as well, and was already deep in conversation with him, from the looks of things.

"Good. You are back," Granny Ivana greeted Mellie and Peter as they walked into his house. "Paul and I have been talking, and I'm almost certain he could be related to my grandfather."

Peter stopped short at his grandmother's announcement. Mellie kept going, hoping the dragon shifter wouldn't take Peter's reaction as some kind of insult. Luckily, Peter's frozen astonishment didn't last too long.

"Are you certain of this?" he asked his babushka.

"Fairly certain, yes," she answered. "We will place calls to the Clan in the morning. There are some written records from my grandfather's time that might be helpful, but I'm almost positive Paul may be descended from my grandfather's sister's line. She was also a dragon, and a beauty, though I only met her once."

"That's one more time than I've ever met any of my blood kin," Paul said, his tone sober. Mellie took a long look at him and realized he was probably trying hard not to get his hopes up too high.

From what little she knew of Paul's background, he'd been raised an orphan under one of the cruelest regimes in modern times. He'd been one of those traumatized Romanian orphans under the Ceausescu regime where the children were neglected, often beaten and lacked basic medical care, clothing and bathing facilities. It was a wonder he'd made it out alive and reasonably sane.

Of course, he was a dragon shifter. If anyone could survive such horrific conditions, it would probably be someone like him, with the fire and magic of a dragon living in his soul. Even if the dragon didn't emerge until puberty, or even later, Paul would have been born with the dual nature inherent in all shifters. It's what probably had saved him.

Still, that kind of experience early in life must have damaged him. At the very least, it had made him wary. Mellie didn't blame him for trying to play it cool with Granny Ivana. As warm as the old woman was, someone who'd been through what Paul had suffered would be wary of anyone new offering the hand of friendship or the promise of family. Granny Ivana was offering both, which must have been a little scary for someone of Paul's background.

Mellie felt the need to say something. She stepped forward to face Paul. This was the first time she'd seen him since the beach. She owed him her thanks at the very least.

"I want you to know that, regardless of whether or not you are related by blood to Peter and his Clan, you will always be welcome here. I have yet to thank you for what you did to make my potion a reality." She stepped a bit closer to Paul and offered her hand. He took it somewhat hesitantly. "I could not have completed my task without you, Paul. Thank you on my behalf and on the behalf of all those you helped protect by your sacrifice."

"It's okay," Paul said quietly, seeming uncomfortable with her praise. "John already thanked me. I'm just glad I was able to help, and really, you did the heavy lifting, Amelia. You are one powerful little witch," Paul's tone warmed as his words became more relaxed.

Now, it was Mellie's turn to feel uncomfortable. "I just did what I had to do," she mumbled.

Paul let go of her hand and smiled. "So did I, S*trega* Ricoletti. So did I."

The fact that he called her by the formal title showed a level of respect that she hadn't expected. Mellie bowed her head in acknowledgement, knowing she was probably blushing at the sudden praise.

Luckily, Peter appeared to have gotten over his shock and came up beside her. He held out his hand to Paul, and they shook hands like old comrades.

"I, for one, hope we can figure out exactly where you fit in the family tree," Peter told the other man.

"You wouldn't mind?" Paul said with painful candor, looking from Peter to Granny Ivana and back again.

"Mind? Who, in their right mind, would argue about having a freaking dragon in the family? I mean, how cool is that?" Peter's enthusiasm was genuine. "I grew up hearing the stories from Babushka about her grandfather, but it was all very hush-hush. We weren't allowed to talk about it outside the family. I was always so curious about him, and about those like him, but I never thought I would actually meet a dragon shifter in my lifetime. I thought they were all gone." Peter's voice grew tight with emotion. "But here you are. Living proof of everything Babushka taught me. I want to claim you as my kin. I want to get to know you and have you learn about your heritage. I want all the things for you that you were denied as a child in a horrible place."

"Why do you care?" Paul asked, his gaze intense, his words brittle with emotion. Mellie held her breath.

Peter reached out and put one hand on Paul's shoulder. "I'm older than you. When you were a boy in that place, I was already a soldier. I saw a little of what went on in Romania under the communist regime of Ceausescu. It was a scandal. It was a tragedy. And, if there had been anything I could do back then to change it, I would have done it."

Paul seemed to crumble a bit as Peter drew him in close. They leaned together, their foreheads touching, two strong men sharing a moment of intense sorrow and joy, all mixed together. It was almost painful to watch, but it was also beautiful.

"I claim you as my kin, Paul Lebchenko," Peter said in a strong voice that carried the weight of a vow. "Even if we can find no record of your people, I know you in my heart. My bear recognizes your spirit. You are my kin, and you will be forevermore part of my family."

Granny Ivana came up beside the men and put one of her hands on each of their bent heads, adding her own benediction. "Blood calls to blood," she intoned. "Zilakov or Lebchenko, bear or dragon, we are the same where it counts. We are Clan."

Then, the old woman took them into her arms as the men turned, one on either side of her. Granny Ivana had one arm around each of them as they hugged her close. It was a touching moment, and Mellie felt the dampness of tears running down her cheeks. Happy tears for a family reunited, never to be lost again.

When Granny Ivana finally released them, all three shifters were sparking with energy. Mellie could see it in the air around them, it was so intense, but it was happy energy. Joyful magic. Happiness given form.

"I hope this means you'll be sticking around Grizzly Cove for a while," Mellie said to Paul.

All three looked at her. "Sorry, love, I didn't tell you," Peter told her. "Paul already decided to stay for a bit. He asked the town council, and we approved. He's got a room at the hotel at the edge of town."

Mellie realized that had probably been decided while she'd been unconscious. "Gee. Sleep a little too long, and all sorts of stuff happens," she groused, her tone teasing. Three smiles answered her. "Well, then. I guess that's settled. Welcome to Grizzly Cove, Paul. I think you're going to like it here."

# # #

ABOUT THE AUTHOR

Bianca D'Arc has run a laboratory, climbed the corporate ladder in the shark-infested streets of lower Manhattan, studied and taught martial arts, and earned the right to put a whole bunch of letters after her name, but she's always enjoyed writing more than any of her other pursuits. She grew up and still lives on Long Island, where she keeps busy with an extensive garden, several aquariums full of very demanding fish, and writing her favorite genres of paranormal, fantasy and sci-fi romance.

Bianca loves to hear from readers and can be reached through Twitter (@BiancaDArc), Facebook (BiancaDArcAuthor) or through the various links on her website.

WELCOME TO THE D'ARC SIDE…
WWW.BIANCADARC.COM

BOOKS BY BIANCA D'ARC

Brotherhood of Blood
One & Only
Rare Vintage
Phantom Desires
Sweeter Than Wine
Forever Valentine
Wolf Hills
Wolf Quest

Tales of the Were
Lords of the Were
Inferno

Tales of the Were – The Others
Rocky
Slade

Tales of the Were – Redstone Clan
The Purrfect Stranger
Grif
Red
Magnus
Bobcat
Matt

String of Fate
Cat's Cradle
King's Throne
Jacob's Ladder
Her Warriors

Gifts of the Ancients
Warrior's Heart

Guardians of the Dark
Half Past Dead
Once Bitten, Twice Dead
A Darker Shade of Dead
The Beast Within
Dead Alert

Grizzly Cove
All About the Bear
Mating Dance
Night Shift
Alpha Bear
Saving Grace
Bearliest Catch
The Bear's Healing Touch
The Luck of the Shifters
Badass Bear
Loaded for Bear

Tales of the Were ~ Grizzly Cove Crossroads
Bounty Hunter Bear

Tales of the Were ~ Were-Fey
Lone Wolf
Snow Magic
Midnight Kiss

Tales of the Were ~ Howls Romance
The Jaguar Tycoon
The Jaguar Bodyguard

Dragon Knights
Maiden Flight
The Dragon Healer
Border Lair
Master at Arms
The Ice Dragon
Prince of Spies
Wings of Change
FireDrake
Dragon Storm
Keeper of the Flame
Hidden Dragons
Sea Dragon

StarLords
Hidden Talent
Talent For Trouble
Shy Talent

Irish Lullaby
Bells Will Be Ringing

Wild Irish
Wild Irish Rose *(Irish Lullaby)*

Sassy Ever After
A Touch of Sass

More than Mated
The Right Spot

Resonance Mates
Hara's Legacy
Davin's Quest
Jaci's Experiment
Grady's Awakening
Harry's Sacrifice

Jit'Suku Chronicles ~ Arcana
King of Swords
King of Cups
King of Clubs
King of Stars
End of the Line
Diva

Jit'Suku Chronicles ~ Sons of Amber
Angel in the Badlands
Master of Her Heart

WWW.BIANCADARC.COM

CPSIA information can be obtained
at www.ICGtesting.com
Printed in the USA
LVOW03s1030080418
572687LV00005B/883/P